Zombie Detective

The Extraordinary Adventures of Sam Melvin

Reviews of *Zombie Turkeys,* Volume 1 of Life After Life Chronicles

"This book will not only make you laugh out loud, you will be surprised at the tender moments! You'll fly right through it and want more. Mr. Zach has a sense of humor we all need!" — Goodreads

"The yarn is fast moving from start to finish, opening with the first attack of carnivorous red-eyed wild turkeys very difficult to kill. They can quickly resurrect after death and grow back cut-off limbs. They're led by a tom full of confidence as Zach gives us this tom's perspectives from time to time as he builds his flock into the tens of thousands throughout Illinois and beyond." —Author Dr. Wesley Britton, BookPleasures.com

"*Zombie Turkeys* is definitely not your typical zombie book. Instead, it is a parody of the standard zombie book, and as such may even be destined for cult status." —Amazon

"I am not one for . . . zombie material, but this was a very entertaining book. The satire kept me reading. Being from Central Illinois, I was quite familiar with much of the locations mentioned in the book. I look forward to what is next." — Amazon

"I loved every gobbling, clucking page of this book. It's this hilarious and insane story that wonderfully hits all the right zombie outbreak tropes I love, but done with turkeys and thanksgiving themes. SO FUNNY! I could read about heroic turkey farmers making chipper-shredder last stands for just about forever!" —Amazon

Reviews of *My Undead Mother-in-law,* Volume 2 of Life After Life Chronicles

"I am a huge zombie fan. I had thought the genre had worked itself out for a while, and then I read this book. I think I have been scarred for life! I foresee months, if not years, of counseling in my future." —Author Greg Aldridge, Goodreads.com

"Who hasn't had mother-in-law issues? Well, what if your mother in law was a zombie?

And yet our hero is a zombie avenging evil with her *Zombie Turkeys*, bulls, and corgis—all under her command. . . . Hilarious and heartwarming at the same time. The perfect wedding shower gift for the new bride. . . . Can't wait for Andy's next adventure!" —Jacqueline Gillam Fairchild, author *Estate of Mind, The Scrap Book Trilogy* – Amazon

"This is the kind of mother-in-law we all need—one who can take over a flock of *Zombie Turkeys* by tearing the lead turkey into bite-sized pieces. This is just as good as *Zombie Turkeys*, folks! Andy Zach is an amazing author! Hope he writes another story soon!" —Amazon

"*My Undead Mother-In-Law,* while not publicized as a YA story, should appeal to a generation for whom blogging is part of their daily life. Zach even asked a less-than-famous blogger to write the humorous foreword to the book. That's really what any reader needs to enjoy this strange yarn—a sense of humor and a willingness to lose yourself in a world that never was and never will be. But a world that seems likely to appear once again in yet another sequel." —Author Dr. Wesley Britton, BookPleasures.com

Reviews of Paranormal Privateers

"Super-fun saga following the antics of the *Paranormal Privateers*. Laugh as they save the world. Who would have thought that the undead would be the saviors of the world? A not-so realistic view of the future of the world. I voluntarily reviewed an ARC of this book. If you like comedy, the paranormal, or books about pirates, you will absolutely love *Paranormal Privateers*." —Ann Keeran Amazon

"*Paranormal Privateers* continues the weirdness with a handful of returning characters and the type of zombies few of us would want to kill, destroy, or dismember. . . . This time around, a crew of zombies has a presidential commission and a super-yacht to take on missions the US military can't. Their leader is the impatient Diane Newby, the undead mother-in-law of the previous volume. . . . All three volumes of the Life After Life series so far are fast-paced romps . . . . . . While not billed as YA novels, I see no reason why young adults wouldn't especially enjoy these yarns. No reader needs to read the previous books to jump into the action.". . . —Dr. Wesley Britton at BookPleasures.com

Reviews of Oops! Tales of the Zombie Turkey Apocalypse

"This is a great book to start with if you haven't tried any Andy Zach book before. It contains stories from both his Life After Life zombie comedy series and his superhero story 'Super Secrets.' It also shows you Zach's sense of humor (plus there's one little horror story that isn't overly gruesome). This book is great for both kids and adults and works just fine on its own. All around, it's a fun collection of tales. 5/5 stars. —Susan from Goodreads

You'd think after three oddball novels . . . that Andy Zach would have exhausted all the comic possibilities in his world of killer *Zombie Turkeys* and superhero zombie humans. You'd be wrong. How about flying zombie pickles? Zombie zucchini?

Zombie caterpillars? . . . How about organizing a zombie worker union at Amazon when zombies can outperform robots? . . . Or zombie residents of a nursing home taking over the place? Oh yeah, there are the aliens who first appeared in *Paranormal Privateers*. . . . The aliens can provide you legal assistance in the form of a sexy avatar who looks exactly like Marilyn Monroe. If you're getting the impression that one Mr. Andy Zach has a wide and wild imagination, you are on the right track. One obvious audience for his quirky tales is the YA readership, especially for all the contemporary references like video gaming and computer lingo. But even grumpy old sixty-somethings like me can have a lot of fun with Andy's characters, scenarios, and plots. . . . Hard to get more original, unique, or surprising than Zach's Life After Life series. Have some fun with Andy Zach! — Dr. Wesley Britton This review first appeared at BookPleasures.com

The Life After Life Chronicles

Andy Zach

Zombie Turkeys

Zombie Detective

My Undead Mother-in-law

Paranormal Privateers

Oops! Tales of the Zombie Turkey Apocalypse

Zombie Detective

Andy Zach

Zombie Detective:
The Extraordinary Adventures of the Sam Melvin

Cover Illustration and jacket design: Sean Patrick Flanagan
Editing: Dori Harrell,
Formatting: Rik Hall
Published by Jule Inc.

PO Box 10705
Peoria, Illinois 61612
zombieturkeys.com
andyzach@andyzach.net
andyzach.net

Library of Congress Control Number: 2021912516
ISBN: 978-0-9978234-6-2

Acknowledgments

Let me begin by acknowledging my illustrator, Sean Flanagan, who designed the covers and the chapter icon. As usual, he delivers more than I expect.

Next is my editor Dori Harrell, who refined my writing while encouraging me even as she corrected my mistakes.

I cannot neglect my next editor, Rik Hall, who performed his usual magic by laying out my book for print and e-book format.

I thank my advanced readers (and fellow authors) Jackie Gillam-Fairchild and Amy Lauder, who gave me valuable feedback on my second draft.

Finally, there is my redoubtable wife, Julie. She patiently listens as I read my clever lines to her, regardless of how lame they may be, and then she positively suggests how the story could be better.

Foreword

Imagine my surprise when I was awoken out of a sound sleep.

"Dashiell! Dashiell Hammett! Are you there?"

"Why are you waking me up?"

"Well, you're dead. And I need to talk with you."

"Oh, now I remember. So what's so important to wake the dead?"

"Andy Zach wants you to write a forward to his book *Zombie Detective*."

"Sounds weird. Why should I?"

"I got you out of a dead sleep for this. Can't you say something?"

"Tell me about it."

"It has a reporter turned detective, Sam Melvin—"

"I like the name Sam. Go on."

"And he solves cases involving zombies."

"Sounds hokey."

"It's meant to be a parody of the detective genre."

"Does anyone die?"

"Yes."

"That's good."

"Andy wants me to read it to you."

BING!

"What's that?"

"My billing meter. Andy has to pony up another fifty bucks. No? Well, bye then, Dashiell."

"Wait! How do I get back to sleep?"

"No problem. You're dead."

Author Dashiell Hammett and Madam Psycho Somantique, medium for the dead

As documented by Andy Zach, who ponied up fifty bucks for a five-minute séance.

**Dedicated to Dashiell Hammett,
creator of Sam Spade**

Contents

I won't play the sap for you.

Sam Spade in the Maltese Falcon

Chapter 1 – Laid Off

"Sam, you're fired." Lisa's green eyes met Sam's brown ones.

"What? Lisa, you and I have worked together at the *Midley Beacon* for ten years! And we've known each other for fifteen! And we've been married almost two months!" Sam broke eye contact, stood up from his desk, and paced about their small office.

"Sorry, Sam. Romance has to take a backseat to finances. Ever since the bottom dropped out of the zombie turkey news market since the first of the year, the *Midley Beacon* hasn't made enough to pay your salary."

"But that's our salary. We share and share alike."

"We can still live on my salary. And you can apply for unemployment now that you're fired."

"But what'll I do all day? I can only play *Fortnite* for so long."

"What did you do before I hired you ten years ago? What did you do while I was in college?"

"Uh, mow lawns. Handyman repair. Stuff like that. But I'm a grown man now. I want more."

"Hmm, you *are* a decent reporter."

"Thanks, Lisa. That's high praise coming from you."

"Well, it's the truth. You've grown from a crappy reporter, like ninety-nine percent of all reporters, to well above average. I did lay off everyone else on the staff before you, you know."

Sam's eyes misted. "Aw, you're making me feel warm and mushy."

"That's part of good management—emotional manipulation."

"Uh, you mean you don't mean it?"

"Nah, I mean it. Emotional manipulation is much more effective if you're sincere. Say, why don't you call Andy Zach and see if he has some royalties to share. We signed a contract with him to get half the royalties from his book *Zombie Turkeus*. We supplied more than half his source material right from the pages of the *Midley Beacon*."

Sam shook his head. "I just called him yesterday. His sales haven't paid for the cover yet, let alone the editing."

"I told him to go with traditional publishing!" Lisa scowled.

"He'd still be trying to get an agent, let alone publishing his book. Who wants to represent a zombie turkey author?"

"So think of something to do with your reporting and investigative skills. That's your first job. Get out of here and work on it at home. When I come home tonight, I want a decision from you. That's a deadline."

"Ok, Lisa. And thanks. You know I work best under a deadline."

"Sure, dear. We'll go out for dinner tonight to celebrate your new career, whatever it will be."

"I'm kind of tired of McDonald's."

"We'll spurge. We'll go to the big city of Peoria. Maybe to the Country Time Buffet."

"Wow. Thanks, Lisa."

"Now, shoo!" Lisa pushed her hands toward him. "Don't forget to clear out your desk."

* * *

After packing his desk into a cardboard box, Sam walked the four blocks from the Midley office to their home at the corner of Maple Street and Main in downtown Midley, Illinois, population five hundred.

Lisa had given him one final assignment. Find a job using his reporting experience.

He set up his laptop and entered "experienced online reporter." He quickly found he should be paid $44,000 to $66,000 a year, depending upon experience. At the peak of the zombie turkey plague, Lisa had paid him $100,000. That lowered to $50,000 and then $25,000 the week before she laid him off.

Sam applied for a dozen jobs online. He didn't feel sanguine. He wanted to talk to someone.

What else could he search for? "Investigator." He'd certainly done that.

Look at that definition. *Private investigator—a person who does not work for the police or government but who undertakes investigations as a subcontractor.*

He sure could do that. He needed a license in Illinois. He met all the qualifications except education and experience. He just had a diploma from Midley High, home of the Midley Meteors.

"Hi, Lisa," he greeted dully when she came home. He hung his head.

"Why are you in a blue funk? Normally you're like a puppy dog when I come home. Didn't you find a job?"

"I really like the idea of being a private investigator, but I need three years experience or a degree, and I've got neither."

"You've got that. You've got ten years experience with the *Midley Beacon.*"

"I can see that, but you're not a private investigator."

"Ha! Running a small-town newspaper is just like being a private investigator. Don't worry about it. I'll get the paperwork done for you, and me and you can start practicing tomorrow."

"Thanks, Lisa, but I don't see how this can work out."

"Let me do the thinking. That isn't your strong suit. Your strength is interviewing and getting people to like you."

"OK, Lisa."

"Now let's go out to celebrate your new private investigator job. I'm thinkin' of chickin."

"Which restaurant?"

"Mama's Chicken in Peoria."

"Mmm-mmm. I can already smell their fried chicken and biscuits!"

"You drive. I'll take my laptop and fill out the online application for a PI agency and a PI license for you."

* * *

The next morning as Sam woke up, Lisa smugly handed him a printed piece of paper. He looked at it, and his mouth dropped open. "Lisa, I can't believe you got me a PI license already!"

"And I'm the proud owner of the Midley Detective Agency—and have been for ten years. I've got the documentation to prove it."

"How could you do that so fast?"

"I've got some friends in the government and all the documentation. Plus, we move at internet speed here at the *Midley Beacon.*"

"But is all that legal?"

"Legal enough to hold up in court. All the documents are back dated. That's all I care about. Don't worry so much, Sam."

"I've got some good news for you. A couple of PI agencies have contacted me. They're from Chicago, Springfield, and St. Louis. Most of them want me to investigate domestic cases or politicians."

Lisa frowned. "Domestic cases are boring. Politicians are too, but at least that's steady work. Start with them and also advertise yourself through the internet. A lot of PI agencies don't. I'll advertise as well. Here's a list of free places to advertise." Lisa handed him a printout.

"Great. Let me kiss you before you go to work."

* * *

Sam took out ads everywhere Lisa suggested, on social media, mailing lists, and local services sites. Then he waited for his phone to ring and email to ding.

Nothing.

He called the PI agencies. They wanted him to have experience with domestic and political investigations. "Thanks, but no thanks," they said.

As he went to sleep that night, Lisa, said, "Don't worry, Sam. Tomorrow will be better."

Soon after Lisa went to work the next day, she called him.

"Sam! I've got a job for you!"

"What is it?"

"There's a possible zombie animal sighting in Normal, Illinois. I just got an email."

"That's not normal."

"Yeah, well, it's right up your alley. Dutchman's Dairy. Here's the address."

Sam drove to Normal in his hulking 1984 Lincoln Town Car. He was glad it'd had bodywork and a new paint job during

4

their prosperous months after the zombie turkey apocalypse. The two-tone brown paint looked spiffy. And it hid rust.

Sam left I-74 after Bloomington and headed to Dutchman's Dairy. Black-and-white cows dotted the green fields around a barn. He parked, then walked to the door and entered.

"Hi. I'm Sam Melvin, private investigator." He'd practiced that opening line on the way over. "I heard you have some sort of zombie animal?"

"Zombie animal?" The middle-aged woman at the counter frowned. Refrigerators full of dairy products lined the walls around the room. "I wonder if Mr. Haagen knows something."

"Who's Mr. Haagen?"

"He's the owner of Dutchman's Dairy."

"And what's your name?"

"I'm Shirley Holzheimer." She picked up her phone and tapped.

"Mr. Haagen? . . . Did you call a private investigator? . . . OK, he's here at the store."

She set her phone on the counter. "He'll be right here."

"Thank you." Sam looked around. Milk. Yogurt. Cheese. Ice cream. Hmmm. Vanilla, strawberry. Maybe Lisa would like a half gallon? He would.

An elderly but spry man entered.

"Mr. Haagen?"

"That's my name—don't wear it out. Or you can call me Steve. You are . . ."

"Sam Melvin, private investigator. I heard you had some zombie animal here."

"Or something. You saw my cows as you came in?"

"Sure."

"Every night for the past week *something* has been breaking through my fence, and my cows have been escaping."

"Wow. Could it simply be your cows getting out?"

"Nope. The fence is broken from outside."

"Um, try a bigger fence?"

"It's electrified. I amped up the voltage. Nothing. I put steel fencing behind the wire. Down it came. I even tried cinderblocks behind the steel fencing. Everything was smashed."

"I guess I'll have to watch it overnight."

"Yeah, I thought of that, and then I thought of you, the famous zombie turkey reporter. I didn't want to try this without your expertise."

"Gee, thanks."

"So you're working as a detective now? A zombie detective?"

"I guess so."

"Well, detect."

Sam went to the broken fence with Steve. A hundred yards of electric fence wire lay on the ground, pointing toward the barn. The steel fencing was bowed and flattened. The cinderblocks were scattered about like cereal pieces from a toddler's high chair.

"Whoa, there was some real force used here."

"I'm glad it's you who's investigating."

"Uh, yeah. What are these tracks all over the ground?"

"My cows. When the fence goes down, they go out. They come back in the same way."

"They return?"

"Sure. They know where the food is."

"What's on the other side of the fence? Who's property is it?

"It's my neighbor's wood lot. We've gone through it together, but we haven't found anything."

"I hope you were armed."

"Yup. We read about the *zombie turkeys*. We had shotguns and flamethrowers. Zombie Burners brand from Amazon."

"That'll do it. I'm not sure the shotguns would help. They only slow them down while they regenerate."

"Heh. I've been reading up on *zombie turkeys*. They're loaded with rock salt."

"That's a new one. I know salt water works on zombie turkeys to kill the bacteria, but I never thought of rock salt."

"You put a load of rock salt into a zombie turkey and what do you get when it dissolves? Salt water."

"That might work."

"We'll find out tonight."

That evening, Sam enjoyed a hearty barbecue steak dinner with Steve and his wife, Abby, around their dinner table. They filled in the cracks with corn on the cob and homemade French fries.

"That was a great meal, Steve, Abby. Thanks."

"I'm glad you enjoyed it, Sam. Seems we always have plenty of beef around here," Abby said.

"Sun's down, Sam. Let's go on our 'steakout.'"

"Ha! Did you get the fence back up?"

"Yup. The boys are getting pretty fast at repairing that baby. I even had them mix up a bag of concrete and pour it over the cinderblocks."

"Would it set that fast?"

"So happens we were laying a new driveway and I got this concrete admixture that hardens it faster. Plus, I had some rebar lying around, and I put that in too."

"Let's see if that slows down this thing, whatever it is."

"You don't think it was those zombie turkeys?"

"No, there'd be turkey feathers everywhere, and they'd attack your cows."

"I didn't know that."

"I'm afraid some other animal has gone zombie."

"Uh-oh."

"Yes. I hope you have your flamethrower."

"Yep. I've got the big one I use to protect the house. I hooked an old well pump to a fifty-five-gallon barrel of napalm. I read about that in the *Midley Beacon*."

"Yes, that was from one of the turkey farmers who survived."

As they settled down in a duck blind to watch the fence from fifty yards away, Sam asked, "Steve, did you have any zombie turkeys out here?"

"Yeah, we got one flock come through before Thanksgiving, but the flamethrower did the trick. I'd say I owe you one, Sam."

They watched the fence in the light of the setting half-moon. Out of the woods galloped a huge shape. Its eyes glowed red. It accelerated and hit the fence head down. Sparks flew as the electric fence wires snapped. The steel fence slammed into the reinforced cinderblocks. The blocks and the concrete cracked and bent but didn't break. The steel rebar held.

"What is that?" Sam cried "It's a zombie *something*."

"I think—" Steve was cut off as the thing slammed into the fence again and again, like a horizontal jackhammer. With each blow, chips of concrete and cinder blocks flew yards from the back of the fence, hitting the blind like shrapnel.

"I think it's going to break through!" Sam said.

The rebar bowed more and more as the concrete and cinderblocks crumbled beneath the massive blows. Then like a spring, a whole section popped out of the gravel that once was solid. The creature followed with a snort and a bellow.

"It's a bull!"

"A zombie bull!"

Simultaneously, they sprayed the huge bovine with their flamethrowers.

Crazed, dazzled, and maddened by the flames, the bull ran in circles and then fled back to the woods. They could trace its path by the burning underbrush in its wake.

"OK, it's time to see if this salt buckshot works." Sam checked the magazine of the shotgun Steve had given him. He found it full and trailed the bull's fiery tracks, carrying the shotgun.

"It worked on the zombie turkeys, but I don't know about this bull."

"There's only one way to find out. Try it. Maybe we'll find it sleeping."

"Wouldn't that be nice."

"Say, Steve, where do you get salt loaded into your cartridges?"

"I do it myself. I've loaded my own cartridges for over forty years."

"I've got the ten rounds you gave me. How much ammo do you have?"

"Another twenty."

"I hope that's enough. I still got my trusty zombie flamethrower."

"You're pretty handy with that shotgun," Steve said as they followed the trail of embers.

"I got a lot of experience with zombie turkeys. Look. The flames are dying out."

"Yeah. There's too much moisture in the ground for them to spread."

"Let me get out my flashlight."

"There are the bull's tracks. No more burnt underbrush."

"Huh. What's this?" Sam picked up a black tattered piece of leather. "What do you think, Steve?"

"That's a piece of the bull. I wondered what would happen to all that burned skin."

"I've seen zombie turkeys burned bald grow skin and feathers back in about ten minutes."

"We've been tracking him for over twenty minutes. Do you think he's recovered?"

"I'd bet on it."

"We're nearly past my neighbor's property and to the next one. There's the property line. And fence."

Sam shone his light on the fence. "There's a bull-sized hole."

Steve examined the broken barbed wire. "It's already starting to rust. It's been broken for at least a week. I check my fence every week. My neighbor doesn't have cows. But maybe he does now."

They went through the breach, hiked down a ravine, and waded across the creek. "Now what? I don't see any tracks," Sam said.

"Me neither. Let's split up. You go downstream toward the road, and I'll go upstream."

Sam followed the rivulet to the road without seeing any tracks. He went back and followed Steve's footprints in the mud next to the creek. He heard nothing. He was so intent on tracking he almost bumped into Steve.

"Hey."

"Shhh." Steve pointed.

Fifty yards away, lying in the mud and watching them, was the bull with red glowing eyes. Was it resting? It snorted.

Sam pointed his shotgun at the bull. "Should we fire?" he whispered.

"Maybe climb this tree first, in case he charges." Steve pointed to a gnarled oak growing in the bank. They clambered to a branch about ten feet above the ground.

"Aim for the head. I don't think we'll get through the hide."

"OK, Steve. One, two, three—"

BLAM! BLAM! The two shots sounded like one. The bull jumped four feet straight up, bellowed, and charged.

BLAM! BLAM!

WHAM! The whole tree shook as the bull rammed it. Sam almost fell but held his shotgun with one hand and a higher branch with another.

"Here he comes again!"

WHAM!

BLAM! BLAM! Click. "I gotta reload, Sam. Brace me."

Sam held his shotgun between his knees, the branch with one hand, and Steve with the other.

WHAM! The bull circled and charged again.

BLAM! BLAM! Sam and Steve took two more shots at the bull's head on the way in.

WHAM!

BLAM! BLAM! Click. Now Sam was out.

This time the bull shook his head, as if annoyed by flies.

"How long did the salt take to dezombify the turkeys?" Sam said as he reloaded his gun.

"Let me think. They were shredded, then grew back feathers, then their eyes turned normal. Maybe fifteen minutes?"

"Let's see. A big turkey might weigh twenty pounds, thirty or forty for a domestic."

"These were domestic birds gone zombie. Big."

"Say the bull weighs two thousand pounds. That's fifty times bigger than a turkey, so he'll need fifty times the salt."

WHAM!

BLAM! BLAM!

"I see a problem, Sam. We've only got thirty cartridges."

"And we've shot ten already."

"Maybe the bull will get bored."

"I wouldn't bet my life on it."

"You might have—"

WHAM!

BLAM! BLAM!

"That was the biggest hit yet, Sam."

"Is the tree tilting?"

"It—"

WHAM!

BLAM! BLAM!

"It's like riding a bucking bronco." Sam loaded his last two cartridges. "I'm out."

"Here's four more." Steve reloaded his gun.

WHAM!

BLAM! BLAM!

"It's definitely tilting."

"I think the roots are pulling out, Sam."

WHAM!

BLAM! BLAM!

They could hear the tree creaking and cracking as it leaned farther and farther. Sam's branch above his head was now behind him. They'd tilted to six feet off the ground.

"Here he comes again!"

BLAM! BLAM! They fired as the bull charged.

WHAM! The tree's limbs hit the creek bank.

BLAM! BLAM! The bull headed off, shaking its bloody head, still red eyed.

Sam reloaded. "I'm out again."

"I've got two left. Plus the four in our guns—we've got six shots left. Let's make them count."

"Look. The tree roots are out of the ground."

"Maybe that'll stop him. We're only five feet off the ground."

"Here he comes, Steve!"

BLAM! BLAM!

WHUMP! The bull rammed the wad of tree roots and earth, flattening the tree into the banks. Their branch was a comfy seat, two feet off the ground. Sam braced his feet on the soil.

BLAM! BLAM! BLAM! BLAM! BLAM! BLAM!

"All gone, Sam."

"Oh, my shoulder!"

The bull shook its head again and trotted off in the moonlight. It lay in the mud, its red eyes stalking them. Slowly they closed as he drifted off to sleep.

"Now what, Steve?"

"Hmmm. I've got a tow chain in my truck. Let's get it and chain him to that tree."

"OK."

With the chain in Steve's hand, they stealthily approached the bull.

"Chain it to the tree first, Sam."

Sam looped it around the stout maple and clipped it to itself.

"I don't think this'll hold a zombie bull," he whispered.

"Mebbe it won't have to. Mebbe it'll be a normal bull now. Let me tie it to the horns."

Steve silently, slowly worked the chain around the bull's horns. He quickly cinched it and snapped it together.

The bull snorted and went on sleeping.

"It's almost dawn. I'll go and check with my neighbor and see if they're missing a bull. You stay here. If he looks like he'll escape, give him the flamethrower."

"Will do."

Sam watched his prey from the tree trunk the bull had knocked down. He bit his lip. If the bull woke up, its zombie strength would make short work of the chain. He looked around for trees and spotted another oak up the bank. He rose, when he heard a snort.

There was the bull glaring at him, tow chain dangling from his horns. With black eyes.

Bull's-eye. He wasn't a zombie anymore. They'd dezombified him.

Chapter 2 – Zombie Detective

"Hello?" Sam answered his cell at his home the next day. He'd written up the zombie bull story and sent it to Lisa. He'd found out the neighbor had fed the bull from a bag of Corn-All grain. Then he'd been busy seeking out zombie stories on the internet so he could try to convince people to hire him. He'd found nothing.

"Hi. Is this Sam Melvin?"

"Yes, this is Sam Melvin, private investigator."

"This is Darin Fowler. Can you look into something for me?"

"Sure. What is it?"

"I found a disemboweled hawk in my yard."

Sam wanted to say "Yuck!" But that would be unprofessional. "Were there scavenger tracks around it? Like a coyote or skunk or possum?"

"No. I heard it hit my awning. I went out, and there it was."

"What do you want me to do? There doesn't seem much to investigate."

"Can you tell if some zombie killed it, like a bat or a rat?"

"Maybe. Do you really want to pay me to investigate this?" Sam felt a stab that this wasn't a good business question. He could hear Lisa yelling at him.

"Oh, I wouldn't be paying you. The government would."

"The government pays for hawk-disemboweling investigations?"

"Sure. I work at the US Fish and Wildlife Service Suboffice here in Marion, Illinois. I have to make sure this was a natural cause and not some person shooting at a hawk."

"Oh. I see." He didn't see at all. Sam had no idea how he could tell. Then he remembered his lifelong friend Bill Westcot, the coroner of Midley, Illinois. Maybe he could help.

"I'll take the assignment. When do you want me there?"

"I'll meet you at my home. That's where it landed yesterday evening. I have it in my freezer in a plastic bag."

"OK. I've got directions to Marion. What's your address?"

"It's 8588 Route 148 Marion, Illinois. That's just down the road from the suboffice."

"I'll be there in about four hours."

"I'll be home and meet you and show you the carcass."

* * *

"Hi, Bill." Sam strolled into the coroner's office on Main Street in Midley.

"Hi, Sam. D'ja come over for a gabfest?" Bill Westcot sounded hopeful, as he stood next to his slab. Bill's smile creased his round blond face.

"Actually, I wondered if you want to go on a field trip to Marion."

"I've got to stay here in case the county sheriff needs me."

"I've going to Marion to determine if a hawk died of natural causes—or unnatural."

"That's pretty weird for you. When did you become a wildlife coroner?"

"When I became a private investigator. I guess weird comes with the job."

"Hmmm . . . You could video conference me in with your phone."

"Do you have the ViewDo video app?"

"Yup."

"I'll use that. I'll call you in four hours or so."

"I'm here until five, Sam."

"Why don't you and Rosie come over for dinner tonight?"

"Sounds good."

"See you, Bill."

"Bye, Sam."

* * *

On the drive through the Illinois plains to Marion, there were enough little towns and trees to break up the monotony of bare winter fields, and the ground grew hillier the farther south he went. He tried to imagine what kind of zombie animal might have killed and eviscerated the hawk. A bat? A zombie bird? He had no clue.

"Entering Marion, Illinois, population seventeen thousand two hundred," Sam read from the sign as he drove into town.

"Take the next left turn to Illinois Route 148. Your destination is on the left," Sam's GPS said.

"Thanks." Sam always felt embarrassed thanking the GPS, but it was automatic.

A small farmhouse stood to the left of the road, surrounded by a cornfield. The wildlife office was to the right.

"It's kind of nice to live across the road from your work," Sam remarked to himself as he pulled into the drive. One good thing about long road trips was he could talk to himself with impunity.

Walking up to the door, he noticed reddish stains on the white aluminum awning. That must be where the hawk had hit.

Before he knocked, the door opened. He was eye to eye with a thin young man with a goatee. He wore a Fish and Wildlife uniform.

"Darin Fowler?"

"You must be Sam Melvin. C'mon in." He opened the door.

"I put the carcass straight into the freezer. Let me get it out for you." Darin led Sam into the basement.

Darin hauled the frozen bird out of the freezer, took it out of the plastic bag, and laid it on a workbench.

"See here? That's where the entrails were ripped out. Do you think it could be a zombie animal?"

"Sure could. Let me get the Midley coroner in on this." Sam conferenced to Bill Westcot.

"Hi, Bill. It's Sam. We've got the bird. Take a look." Sam gave Bill a close-up of the bird's ripped belly.

"Hmmm. Very interesting. Zoom in on the edges."

Sam moved the phone until it almost touched the edges of the ragged tear. He found the zoom feature on his camera and expanded the image to an almost microscopic level.

"That tears it." Bill's voice came out of the phone. "Those are definitely claw marks along the edges. Do you see the lacerations along the skin, digging down into the viscera?"

"Uh, yeah."

"So what kind of animal was it?" Darin asked.

"Small but with strong claws," Bill replied.

"Was it a zombie? Wait. I guess it has to be."

"Why do you say that?" Sam asked Darin.

"Small animals hit by a hawk's stoop usually die instantly. The claws break the neck. If that doesn't do the trick, they bite them in the neck."

"Now you're in my area of expertise. Coming back from the dead is a sign of zombiism. I can't count how many zombie turkeys I've killed—and seen them rise again."

"So what do we do now?"

"Hmmm. Some small zombie animal, suitable for hawk food. Probably a rabbit. Let's go wabbit hunting!" Sam used his best Elmer Fudd voice.

"Do rabbits even become zombies?"

"Yes," answered Sam and Bill Westcot simultaneously.

"Go ahead, Sam."

"According to Dr. Galloway of the Northwestern University Poultry Research Institute—"

"Also known as the 'Turkey Institute.'" Bill smiled on the cell screen.

"Right. That was funny the first time. Maybe the first dozen times. Not now. Anyway, Dr. Galloway tried to induce zombiism into all kinds of animals during the turkey apocalypse. Rabbits were one of the animals that became zombies. Darin, do you have a tracking dog? And a shotgun?"

"I've got a shotgun. I like to duck hunt—in season, of course. My friend Mike has a tracking dog. I'll call him."

"Thanks for your help, Bill. Is there anything more you've got to say or see before we take off?"

"Just be careful, Sam. You're the only friend I've got left from elementary school."

"Yeah, I won't underestimate the rabbit. We've got shotguns, my flamethrower, and a bucket of salt water too."

"Good."

"See you, Bill."

"Bye."

Darin put his phone away and said, "Mike said we can borrow his dog. He'd come, but he's working. The dog, Prince, knows me and is a great rabbit hunter. What's the deal with the salt water? I know salt water knocks out zombiism, but how will we get the rabbit into the water?"

"We'll shoot it, pick it up, and dunk it in."

"Sounds good. We just have to make sure it doesn't disembowel us."

"Right. That's why we got these." Sam brandished his 12-gauge shotgun, loaded with 00 shot. He knew it worked on zombie turkeys. It took them over fifteen minutes to regenerate enough to stand up. He didn't think a bunny would do any better.

They patrolled the fields around Darin's house in a spiral, looking for a rabbit warren. Prince barked, sniffed, and wagged enthusiastically.

"This is the first time I've ever been nervous about hunting a rabbit," Darin said as he wandered through tall grass.

Suddenly Prince barked. He pointed at a tree.

"That's a squirrel, Prince."

"Uh, Darin, look at the squirrel."

"What? Oh, it has red eyes."

"Hold Prince." Sam aimed at the squirrel with the shotgun. BLAM!

The squirrel flew backward about ten feet and landed belly up.

"Ew. There's not much left of it, Sam."

"That's why squirrel hunters don't use double-aught buckshot. Unless they're zombie squirrels. Look. The wounds are closing. Let's hustle back to the house with the squirrel and baptize it in the salt water."

Sam picked the squirrel up by the tail and headed toward the house. Darin jogged with him.

The squirrel twitched. Sam glanced at it. All the holes were healed. This wasn't good.

He dropped the squirrel on the ground, chambered another round, and gave it a blast. BLAM!

Too late. The squirrel jumped ten feet and hit the ground running. Prince barked and took off after it. It ran up a tree, then came out on an upper branch. *Chitter! Chitter!*

"I guess it told you," Darin said.

"I'd be mad, too, if I were shot by a shotgun."

"So what do we do now? Blast away?"

"Yes and no. Let me try this round." Sam pulled out two shells from his vest pocket.

"What's written on them?"

"It says 'Morton.' These are rock-salt charges I got from my previous zombie adventure." Sam loaded the two shells into his gun.

"Is it effective? Sorry for all the questions, but this zombie stuff is all new to me."

"No problem. Everyone starts from ground zero. Yep, it worked on a zombie bull—eventually." Sam aimed at the squirrel.

BLAM!

The squirrel fell from the tree to the ground, landed on its feet, and climbed the tree again.

BLAM!

The squirrel ran back to the tree and then collapsed.

Sam walked over and picked it up again by its tail. Its coat was shredded and bleeding, but it was still alive, quivering and trembling.

"Crap. I feel crummy for shooting a zombie squirrel."

"Better it than you. Remember the hawk."

"Right. Let's give you a proper baptism." They jogged back to Darin's house, and Sam dunked it in the five-gallon bucket.

It spluttered awake, and Sam let it go on the ground. It shook all over and ran up a tree. *Chitter! Chitter!* it scolded. But its eyes were now black.

"That's that," Sam said. "Now, you said the government will pay me?"

"Yup. I'll pay you out of the pest control budget. Come over to my office across the road and I'll write you a check."

* * *

Sam had to stop at the *Midley Beacon* office and tell Lisa the good news. He entered the door on Main Street.

"Lisa! Good news!"

"Don't yell, Sam. I can hear you fine." Lisa looked up from her laptop.

"Sorry. I'm excited. I got a thousand dollars, paid by the State of Illinois." Sam handed her his check.

"Great! So you listened to me and raised your price from six hundred dollars per day to one thousand dollars? Now, I've got some good news for you."

"What's that?"

"I decided to rent a portion of the *Midley* office to you as detective space. I'll add 'Zombie Detective Agency' to our sign as well. You never know when you might get walk-in business."

"Thanks, Lisa."

"Normally I'd rent the space for a hundred dollars a day, but since you're family, I'll only charge you fifty."

"Uh, thanks?"

"That's assuming you'll answer the zombie turkey hotline. I'm busy running the paper."

"Mm, OK."

"Finally, I got this gift for you." Lisa handed him a small gift-wrapped package.

"Thanks, Lisa! I can't imagine what it is."

"I'm not surprised."

Sam opened the package. It was a brass nameplate engraved "Sam Melvin, Zombie Detective."

"Aw, Lisa." He hugged and kissed her.

"And here's the real surprise."

"What?"

Lisa went to the coat closet and brought out a brand-new fedora.

"Try it on, Dick Tracy."

"It fits perfectly! This calls for another, better kiss."

"Mmmm." When they came up for a breath, she said, "I have to tell you: I'm really proud of you, Sam. Your first two days, two successful cases, and sixteen hundred dollars. Few new detectives can say that."

"Why don't we go home so we can properly celebrate?"

"Without being celibate." They laughed.

Chapter 3 – Vegan Inc.

The next morning Sam set up his laptop at his old desk and powered up. His thirty-year-old garbage-picked office chair had never felt so good. Across the fifteen-foot-wide office, he could see Lisa scowling at her computer screen, as usual.

Lisa glanced up and transferred her scowl to him. "Why aren't you working?"

"Just getting started. You're such a distraction." Sam smiled.

"Hmph! Maybe you should turn and face the wall." But her heart wasn't in it. Sam thought she was pleased.

Email first, in case he got a case. Quickly he deleted thirty advertisements, marking them as spam. There was a newsy note from Steve Haagen saying the bull was doing fine and still non-zombie.

What was this? *"Urgent! Open immediately?"* Sounded like another spam.

Sam read the email.

> *February 17, 2016 2:13 AM*
>
> *Dear Mr. Melvin,*
>
> *I have a super-urgent matter to discuss with you, using your expertise. It's too complex for email. Please call me ASAP when you get in.*
>
> *Bryce Butterworth*
> *Geneticist, Vegan Inc.*
> *Fort Wayne, IN*

(260) 234-8297

He dialed the number.

"Hello, Bryce Butterworth, Vegan Inc."

"Hi, Bryce, this is Sam Melvin, I just read your email, and I'm curious about what's so urgent."

"Sam! I'm so glad you called. We're in crisis mode here. Come immediately to Fort Wayne and help us here at Vegan Inc. I'll advance you your daily fee by PayPal."

"OK. That's great. But what's the problem?"

"Simply put, it's an animal infestation we can't handle."

"What kind? Are they zombies?"

"Uh, maybe."

"You don't know? What kind of animals?"

"It's kind of hard to explain . . . You'll just have to come here and see for yourself."

"I'll be in Fort Wayne in about four hours."

"Sam!" Lisa interrupted. "Use the *Midley* plane. It'll save you three hours."

"Oh, I forgot. I probably could have used that for Marion. Bryce, I'll come by private plane. I'll see you in about two hours."

"That's great. I'm sending you the money now. Bye."

"So you got another case. Did I hear correctly that he's sending you the money by PayPal?"

"Yes." Sam was used to Lisa eavesdropping on his phone conversations. He didn't have anything to hide from her.

"Fantastic. I'll invoice you for the cost of the plane and pilot. Do you have Dan Cosana's number?"

"Yup. I'll call him now."

* * *

An hour and fifteen minutes later, Dan and Sam landed in Dan's Turbo Arrow at the Fort Wayne Allen county airport. Sam was tickled to wear his fedora on an assignment.

"It's good to fly with you again, Dan."

"Yes, I miss you and Lisa. Business a bit slow?"

"It was, but it's picking up."

"Great. I'll stay in a hotel by the airport until you're ready to go. Just call me."

"Will do."

Sam picked up his rental car and drove to Vegan Inc. Fort Wayne was the world headquarters for the agricultural giant, a key competitor with Corn-All.

A slender young man with blond tousled hair entered the visitors' center. "Sam Melvin?"

"Yes. Bryce Butterworth?"

"That's me. Let me give you a briefing before I take you to the problem. Nice hat, by the way."

"Thanks. My wife gave it to me."

They sat in a nearby conference room. "How much do you know about Vegan Inc., Sam?"

"They're a big ag firm that competes with Corn-All. They provide garden seeds for farmers and home gardeners. They sell a line of vegetables. That's about it."

"Right. I was recently tasked with a secret project to diversify into pig breeding."

"OK. That's a big leap."

"Yes. It was high risk, high reward, so they threw it to me. I'm fresh from college and too dumb to know something is impossible."

"So where do I come in?"

"Let me finish with the background. We wanted a fast-growing, healthy strain of pigs. I thought, *Wouldn't it be great if they grew as fast as zombie turkeys?*"

"Uh-oh."

"Right. I created a pig modified with zombie turkey and hippo and mouse DNA."

"What?" Sam's stomach clenched.

"I won't go into all my failures with other combinations. This one worked. I get pigs that grow from piglets to full grown in four weeks."

"But what's the catch?"

"They look like hippos. And they grow only to about one pound."

"Sounds more like a failure than a success."

"They do taste like pork. And they reproduce fast enough to make up for their lack of size. But—" Bryce stopped and sighed.

"Tell me the worst."

"They escaped my lab. They're infesting the whole building. People keep finding them in the toilets. It's very upsetting."

"Are they zombies?"

"No, I couldn't get that to work with pigs, hippos, or mice."

"Whew. That's a load off my mind. Sounds like you need pest control."

"Right. I couldn't find any who would tackle it, so I called you."

Sam rubbed his head. "I don't know, Bryce."

"You're my last hope. If you don't catch them all, I'm fired."

"OK, I'll give it a try. Just tell me one thing. Why is Vegan experimenting with pigs? Isn't that against their image of a pure vegan, non-GMO food source?"

"Well, yes. That's why the project was top secret. If I can get it to work, it'll be a spin-off company, Perfect Pork."

"All right. Let me take a look at the hippo-pigs, or whatever you call them."

"Right now I'm calling them micro-hippos, but I'm sure the marketers will think of something more appealing." Bryce stood. "Let's go to the restroom."

"You have to go?"

"No, that's the quickest way to find them."

They walked in. "Check every stall and toilet."

Sam looked in the first toilet. A cute hippo looked at him and then disappeared down the drain with a swirl.

"I found one!"

"Good. Now let's go to the cafeteria. That's where they feed."

"Yuck."

"Right. That's one more reason why we need you."

Lunch hadn't started, so there were just a few people scattered across the large cafeteria.

"First, we'll go to the salad bar. Ah. They've been here. Don't step in the hippo droppings."

"How do they get up to the salad bar?"

"They climb as well as mice. Their feet are the least hippo-like. They're more like rats or mice." Bryce stirred the salad greens, then the fruit salad. Out popped two eyes peering above the strawberries, pineapple, and melon.

"Grab it, Sam!" Bryce whispered.

Snatching a pair of tongs, Sam nabbed the tiny pest and hauled it from the bowl of fruit.

"Squee! Squee!"

"Gotcha! Oh no you don't!" Sam held on to the crossbreed with both hands on the tongs.

Bryce ran and grabbed a plastic bucket from the kitchen. Sam dropped the animal into it.

Thump!

"Heavy little bugger. Look at him climb!" Sam marveled as the hippo's ratlike claws scrambled up the vertical plastic.

Bryce slammed a lid on the bucket. "Don't I know it!" Then he grabbed the bowl of fruit from the salad bar. "I don't think this'll be appreciated."

"Whatcha going to do with it?"

"Pitch it."

"Don't. I've got an idea."

"What's that?"

"We can use it as bait."

"That may work. What kind of trap should we use?"

"A live-catch trap, like for raccoons."

Bryce put down the bowl. "Let me see how many we got at our local Farm and Fleet." He dialed.

"Hi. Do you have a live animal trap? . . . About one to two pounds, like a large squirrel. . . . How many do you have? . . . All right, put them aside for me. I'll be right over to pick them up." He turned to Sam. "They've only got five. Why don't you drive me over, and I'll order more over the internet?"

"Glad to do it!"

They were back in half an hour and baited the five traps in bathrooms, the cafeteria, and the kitchen. Then they ate.

"I don't know if I can eat the fruit salad." Sam sat down, eyeing the bowl on his tray.

"Don't worry. I saw them make it while I put the trap in the kitchen. I can hardly eat. I'm eager to see if this works."

Sam wolfed down his hamburger. "We can go and check now."

All the bathroom traps had caught hippos. Sam carried three full traps back to the cafeteria. One of them had two hippos in it.

"I've got four," he told Bryce as he came out of the cafeteria carrying two traps.

"Me too. Let's take them to my lab. I've got a safe enclosure there."

"When will the other traps arrive?"

"Tomorrow. I ordered them next-day delivery."

"How many did you order?"

"A hundred."

"How many hippos are out there wandering this building?"

"I had twenty escape, and several were pregnant. They reproduce like rabbits, having ten to twenty per litter."

"How long ago did they escape?"

"Two weeks ago. We could have a hundred or more."

"What's the gestation period?"

"Two weeks."

Sam and Bryce captured twenty more hippos before the end of the day.

The next day Sam drove in early and helped Bryce set out the hundred new traps. They caught over a hundred hippos. By the end of the day, all the traps had been empty for hours.

"We'll probably pick up another dozen or so. Thanks, Sam. You've been worth every penny Vegan has paid you."

"Do you need an invoice?"

"Just for your trip expenses. I've been paying you a thousand dollars per day, your standard rate."

"It's great doing business with you! Let me know if you ever get any other weird animal infestations."

"Maybe you can help me get rid of a hundred or so micro-hippos."

"Hmm. Let me give Andy Zach a call. He's got info on all kinds of odd animals." Sam speed-dialed Andy.

"Hi, Andy. How are sales going on *Zombie Turkeys*? . . . Almost breaking even? That's great. I've got a little problem. No, make that a hundred and twenty-seven little problems. We've got a micro-hippo infestation. . . . That's right. They weigh about a pound or two. The question is, how do we get rid of them? . . . That might work. We'll give it a try. Thanks! Bye."

"What's the good word?"

"Andy thinks you can sell them as pets."

"That's a great idea! I might even get a promotion for this. At least I won't be fired now."

* * *

Sam typed up his trip report on the flight home. It was what professional detectives did after each case. Also, Lisa said she'd buy his stories for the *Midley Beacon*. Her paying him was kind of like taking money from one pocket and into another, but it made her happy. She always smiled when she could reduce their taxes.

His phone played *Lord of the Rings*, Lothlorien theme.

That was Lisa's ring. Sam always thought of Lisa as like Galadriel: powerful and beautiful.

"Hel—"

"Sam! Drop whatever you're doing and get to Hagerstown, Maryland. I've got the Maryland governor breathing down my neck, and you're the one she wants."

"Why? What's going on?"

"Some kind of zombie turkey outbreak. I'm sure it'll be a piece of cake for you."

"Thanks, Lisa."

"What's up with Vegan Inc? Did you get their infestation cleared up? Do you have a report for me?"

"I'm just finishing it. It'll be on its way in five minutes."

"Great. We need to fill the *Midley Beacon* with quality content, and you give the best."

"Aw, Lisa."

"It's only the truth. Stop by home before you leave for Hagerstown. I'd like to see you."

"Ditto, Lisa!"

"We've got two hours before your flight out, which I booked at the *Midley Beacon*'s expense. Let's use the time productively."

Chapter 4 – Turkeys

Sam sighed contentedly.

"Me too. Now that's over, let's talk business. About Maryland."

"What's going on, Lisa?"

"After the zombie turkey apocalypse, they kept a flock of wild zombie turkeys for hunters. Maryland's gotten great tourist trade from that. The recent bad weather on the East Coast has kept the hunters down, and the turkeys are out of control. They're hunting people in the suburbs of Hagerstown."

"What can I do about that? That's a problem for the National Guard. I'm a lover, not a fighter."

"Yes, I know. The governor, Mary Landis, called me begging for your help. They can't find the turkeys. I promised her that you've got a nose for zombie turkeys and you'll find their hideouts in no time flat. They're paying you two thousand per day for this, so don't screw up. I've booked an evening flight to Hagerstown from the Peoria airport at six p.m. That gives you an hour to get there. Starting now."

"I guess I'd better get dressed."

"I'll put your computer and bags in your car. Here's the governor's phone number. Give her a call on your way."

* * *

Sam settled into his first-class seat as the chartered jet climbed. *This is nice.* The state of Maryland was paying his expenses, so Lisa went all out. He called the governor of Maryland, Mary Landis.

"This is Governor Landis. Who is this? How did you get my cell number?"

"Hi, Governor. I'm Sam Melvin, a private investigator. I got your number from Lisa Melvin, my wife."

"I'm so glad you called, Sam. You surprised me for a second. I thought it was a spam call. I'm delighted you're coming. These zombie turkeys are a real problem in the suburbs. People are afraid to go out."

"Are they coming out in the morning?"

"Yes, and attacking people as they go to work."

"Why haven't you been able to find them?"

"We're using dogs, but with the heavy snow on the ground, it's hard finding and tracking them. For zombie turkeys, we have a year-round open-hunting season, and the hunters keep their numbers down. We've had snow on the ground since November, and storms have closed the airports several times."

"Hmmm. This reminds me of the Illinois National Guard trying to find them. The Northwestern University Poultry Institute discovered that turkeys hibernate after a heavy meal. Their body temperatures drop to the air temperature. Have they eaten any people?"

"Just between you and me, hundreds. That's not for public knowledge. And that's not counting the dogs, cats, and goats they've eaten."

"Huh. Seems serious. Where are they attacking in the state?"

"By Hagerstown, near the Pennsylvania border."

"Let me pull up a topological map of Maryland. That's how I tracked them in Illinois."

"Let me tell you, Sam, I'm one of your biggest fans. I read every news story you wrote."

"Uh, thanks! Let's take a look at Hagerstown. Whoa! You've got a lot of rivers and trees around there. That's where zombie turkeys like to live. Have they been attacking the western suburbs?"

"Uh, yes. How'd ya know?"

"The creeks and woods are where zombie turkeys love to hide. Have you checked those areas?"

"Uh, I think so. Let me contact my National Guard. I'll get back to you."

"OK. Bye."

"Bye."

* * *

It was snowing when Sam landed at Hagerstown airport. The plows scurried back and forth, keeping the runways clear.

Approaching the rental car counter, Sam said, "I'd like your best four-wheeler."

"Oh, that'd be our Ford Raptor. That'll be a hundred ninety-nine per day or eleven hundred per week."

"OK. Here's my card. This'll work well for hunting?"

"You bet. Where are you hunting?"

"Oh, in the parks around Hagerstown?"

"Whatcha huntin'?"

"Turkeys. zombie turkeys."

"Oh, you might want a Hunt Master too."

"What's that?"

"A small eight-wheeled vehicle. It'll go anywhere. In dense brush, you won't be able to take the truck. Here's a picture." The clerk showed him his phone screen.

"Ooo! That's cool. Where do I rent one of those? Here?"

"Just a minute." The rental agent tapped his screen and then held his phone to his ear. "Justin? Yeah, it's Ryan. Could you send over your Hunt Master to the rental office here at the airport, right away? I've got a rental customer who wants one. Great."

"So you're getting one here? When will it be here?"

"In about half an hour. My friend Justin runs a hunting store, and he rents them out."

Sam paid for the rental and familiarized himself with the Raptor while he waited. He loved big cars and trucks. This one had a raised suspension and 400 horsepower. That was the same as his Lincoln.

A truck pulled up. The Hunt Master started up and pulled out of the pickup bed and up into his.

Finally, he was off on his great turkey hunt. He headed off in the dark winter evening to join up with the Maryland National Guard.

* * *

He felt great. His flock was bigger than ever. Every morning he led his flock from the woods to the hard paths to sate their hunger with tasty predators. He looked at the lightening sky. Time to feed again.

* * *

"What can I do for you, sir?" The clean-cut National Guardsman said with a snap as Sam entered the National Guard lobby holding his fedora in his hand.

"Hi. I'm Sam Melvin, zombie detective. I'm here to help with your zombie turkey infestation."

"Great! I'm sure the captain will be glad to see you." He picked up his phone. "Captain Carpenter? A Mr. Sam Melvin is here for the zombie turkeys." He gestured. "You can go right in that office."

A square, average-height man stood behind his desk, looked Sam straight in the eye, and shook his hand. "Mr. Melvin, I'm glad to see you."

"Thank you, Captain Carpenter."

"We've cruised all over this valley looking for these turkeys, and we haven't made a dent in them. At least we've cut down on their predation of civilians by culling their numbers and being a buffer around the populated areas."

"I hope so. Are you tracking the number of homeless? They're the first to go in a zombie turkey outbreak."

"Uh, no. But there are fewer in the winter. They go into public shelters, like the Salvation Army or the YMCA."

"How about hunters?"

"Yes, we've lost quite a few of those. They'll shoot the zombie turkeys they want, then get attacked going home with their birds. They hold them off until they run out of ammo. Not good."

"Yep. That's why I use my trusty turkey-incinerator flamethrower. Don't leave home without it."

"That matches our standard zombie turkey operational protocol—to stop them with fléchettes and then clean them out with flamethrowers."

"Let's get hopping or sledding or mushing through the snow tonight while they sleep. Do you have your K-9 corps ready to go?"

"We have multiple units working twenty-four seven. The next one starts at ten, in twenty minutes."

"Let's go! I'm eager to try out my Hunt Master eight-wheel drive."

"I saw that in the back of your truck. You may be able to reach places we cannot. We use MRAPs in the woods and then go out on foot when our dogs signal they've found something."

"Show me where you've searched so far."

The captain put up a map on the wall-sized video screen. It was dotted with little black symbols and bigger red ones. Looking closely, Sam saw they were miniature turkeys.

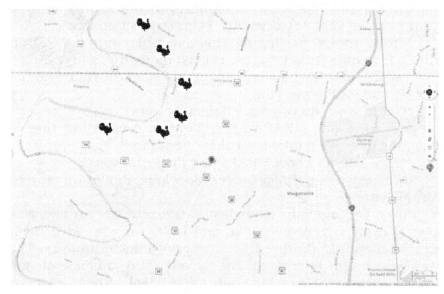

"The small black symbols are where we've found turkeys. The large red ones are where we fought them. The battles are all on the west side of Hagerstown. And so are all the turkeys we've found in the woods."

Sam walked to the screen and peered closely at the symbols. "Hmmm. Look at the turkey attacks, Captain. Do you see the pattern?"

"It's kind of a semicircular tangent to Hagerstown. What does that mean?"

"See this attack near Cearfoss Pike? Then this one on Fairview Road? Look how they follow the Conococheague Creek. All these attacks in Fairview Acres—it's surrounded by a big loop of the creek."

"So they're following the creek."

"Yes. Even zombie turkeys need water. And I'm sure there are lots of trees and brush around it."

"So much so we haven't bothered investigating the banks."

"That's where we'll go then."

"Let's meet Lieutenant Michael Avery. He'll lead the night shift."

"OK. Let me get into my overalls and hunting gear."

The guardsmen loaded Sam's Hunt Master vehicle into the MRAP while Lieutenant Avery and Sam discussed their plans.

"The Guard has snow machines, but not in this state. If your hunting vehicle works out, I can requisition a few."

"I'm a rookie at driving this machine, but I've driven through zombie turkeys in my car too many times to count."

"We'll use you as a scout. If you're attacked, return to the MRAP, and we'll cover you."

"Got it. Now, do you have flamethrowers?"

"We have one MRAP with a flamethrower rather than a machine gun. We'll take it for this operation."

"Huh. I didn't know MRAPs had flamethrowers."

"We keep some things secret. So where should we search, Mr. Melvin?"

"Just call me Sam. Your last battle with the turkeys was over here by Greencastle Pike and I-70. You shredded them with fléchettes and drove them away with flamethrowers. The turkeys would retreat to the woods and bushes of the Conococheague Creek to hide and heal. They may go downstream to the Chesapeake and Ohio Canal National Historical Park by the Potomac River. We'll follow the bank downstream to the Potomac and then go upstream."

"Sounds good. I'll bring along two K-9 specialists to cover both sides of the river. Now let's get you fitted out with night vision goggles and a comm unit."

"I'll feel like a real special-ops guy."

"You are. Zombie turkey ops."

The six-wheeled MRAP rumbled down Greencastle Pike. They turned down Kemps Mill Road and pulled off next to the Conococheague Creek. Sam hopped out and drove his Hunt Master off the trailer.

The K-9 handler, Sergeant Jeff Swanson, sat next to him. "I'll send Jimmy to sniff out the turkeys.

"Why do you call him 'Jimmy'? That's an odd name for a dog."

"It's because he has a great nose, like Jimmy Durante."

"Ha."

Amy Bradley hopped in behind them. "I'll take Chino across the creek."

"And why do you call him Chino?"

"I like wearing chino fabric."

"OK. Off we go!" Sam gunned the engine, and the eight wheels threw up snow as they plowed along the creek bank. Amy directed Chino to check the far bank.

After a hundred yards Jimmy signaled he'd found something.

Sam pulled over, while Jimmy dug furiously. Snow and dirt flew. Amy brought Chino over to help. Soon the dogs uncovered a very dirty and very comatose turkey.

"It looks dead," Jeff said.

"It's hibernating. zombie turkeys do that after a big meal and to heal up." Sam brought out his bowie knife from his belt sheath and cut the turkey in half and then in quarters. "No more regenerating for you, bird."

"Chino's signaling."

The dogs soon dug out another, and then three more turkeys.

"That's only five out of thousands," Sam said as they climbed back into the Hunt Master.

They arrived at the Potomac River and the park area. The MRAP followed them on the road.

"I'll take Chino across the river." Amy dog-trotted to the bridge, Chino wagging behind her.

Sam and Jeff followed the snowy river bank on the east side of the river. Traffic on I-70 whooshed past them.

"We haven't looked this far off the road in our earlier searches." Jeff watched Jimmy leaping and plunging through the snow.

Sam followed his gaze. "There's at least one of us having great fun."

Jimmy alerted with a short, sharp bark.

"That was fast. Let's see if we can fit between these bushes. Watch your head, Jeff."

Jimmy pointed at a human skeleton.

"Ewww. I've seen what zombie turkeys can do, and I still get grossed out." Sam shuddered.

"Let's see if we can identify this poor guy. By his gear, he's a hunter." On his comm, Jeff said, "We need a body bag." He grunted and looked at Sam. "One of the guys will run one out to us."

"You guys brought body bags?"

"Yup, a dozen. We've learned we need them."

Jimmy barked again.

"That's a turkey bark."

"I'll get him. Do you mind handling this guy's corpse? I'm embarrassed to say I can't take this."

At Jimmy's direction, Sam unearthed six more turkeys from hibernation and cut them up. He listened on the comm as Jeff identified the hunter as Thomas Plankworth from Hagerstown, age sixty-one. Across the Potomac, Amy and Chino found twenty turkeys hibernating and dispatched them.

Once the body was bagged and tagged, they continued upstream. After killing hundreds of hibernating turkeys later, they got a comm: "All units proceed to MD-40. Major turkey attack underway in Cearfoss, Maryland."

"Crap. That's past their previous attack in Fairview Acres. They're getting closer to Hagerstown," Jeff said.

Sam gunned the engine, and they mushed uphill to the access road where the MRAP awaited them. Jimmy trotted behind them. Another MRAP picked up Amy.

Sam drove a quarter-mile into the woods, when the first zombie turkey flew into his face, spurs first. They scratched the tough Plexiglas on his helmet.

"Gobble! Gobble!"

Sam speared the bird on his twelve-inch knife and continued to plow toward the MRAP. Hundreds of turkeys descended from the trees. Sam ran over some, pounding them into the snow. Jeff shot them with his M4 carbine. Sam again gunned the engine as he hit level ground. The flock followed them, pecking at their backs, as they hunkered down on the eight-wheeled vehicle.

Sam had often thought zombie turkey victims looked like they had been assaulted by hundreds of pickaxes. Now he felt their beaks cut through his parka, slowly bleeding him to death. The cold air congealed his blood quickly. Next to him,

Jeff had fixed a bayonet on his M4 carbine and sliced wildly, beating off the turkeys.

He saw the MRAP ahead and sped toward it. The flamethrower shot liquid flame over his head. He felt the heat on his exposed bloody skin.

Weak and faint from blood loss, Sam parked next to the MRAP as the flames shot out overhead. Jeff jumped out and opened the rear of the vehicle. Sam fell off into the soft snow between the vehicles. His last sight before losing consciousness was a huge tom turkey stalking toward him.

"Gobble! Gobble!"

* * *

He led his flock to a feeding spot. A predator zoomed by the flock, but not fast enough to escape them. He didn't worry about how the predators moved so fast—he just led his turkeys to food.

A metal box shot out fire. He didn't like fire, but he had the predator's blood in his mouth, and he couldn't stop feeding. He walked toward the predator.

"Gobble! Gobble!"

* * *

"Crap on a stick!" Jeff reloaded his M4 carbine and shot the turkey pecking at Sam's back. It flew backward, staggered up, and stumbled away.

"No getting away today, you turkey." Sighting carefully, he blew off its head and put three more rounds into the body. It plopped over, making a red Rorschach blotch on the snow.

He checked Sam. He couldn't tell if he was breathing or if he had a heartbeat. He moved him to the MRAP and called the medics. They were in a medical truck near Cearfoss. Jeff dressed Sam's oozing, ragged wounds as the MRAP got underway. Sam seemed barely alive.

"Step on it, Fred. Sam needs a transfusion." Their driver, specialist Private Zagreb, accelerated to their maximum speed of sixty miles per hour on Cearfoss Pike. They saw flocks of turkeys flying into the town and heard the crackle of firearms up ahead.

"Gobble! Gobble!"

"There are thousands of them," Lieutenant Avery said. "Hold fire on the flamethrower until I give the signal."

"That's the medic truck we need." Jeff pointed out the window. A block from the tiny township sat an MRAP with a red cross on its side.

Fred skidded next to the medical MRAP. Out came two soldiers carrying a stretcher. Jeff helped them slide Sam onto the stretcher.

The sky grew dark. Jeff looked up into a solid mass of zombie turkeys descending on them.

"Gobble! Gobble!"

"Run!"

"Lieutenant! Can we fire—"

"Fire! Soldiers, cover the men going to the truck."

The flamethrower spewed death on either side of the three men carrying Sam to the medic truck. Flaming balls of turkeys fell from the sky, melting the snow where they hit. Still, dozens pecked at the men as they raced to the truck.

The two riflemen in the MRAP picked off any turkeys that came close to them.

A bullet whizzed by Jeff's ear as he carried the back half of the stretcher.

"Faster!" He pushed the two medics into the truck with the stretcher and jumped in after them. They slammed the doors closed.

Too late. One large zombie turkey had followed them in, flapping, gouging with its spurs, and pecking with its beak.

Jeff pulled out his belt knife and stabbed it. It didn't slow down or seem to notice, but it began pecking at him.

One medic whipped out a scalpel and cut off its head. Blood spurted like a garden hose. The neck still tried to peck Jeff, but only left him bloody. He stabbed it through the chest and hacked it into two. The giblets and blood spilled onto the floor like ghastly gravy. The two sides quivered and convulsed for a minute and then died.

The medic looked at his bloody scalpel. "I think I'm going to have to disinfect this." Then he looked around the gory interior. "And the operating room."

"Ya gotta give Sam a blood transfusion. I think he's in shock."

"Yeah, sure. Too bad we can't give him turkey blood." The medic, Herb, hung a bag of blood above Sam. He swabbed his arm with disinfectant and expertly inserted the needle into his vein.

"Put all his stuff in here." Herb held open a garbage bag.

"I'd better double bag this." Jeff wrinkled his nose at Sam's bloody, shredded parka.

Sam already looked better when Jeff left for his MRAP. Jimmy was waiting for him and nuzzled his hand with a bloody muzzle.

"Good boy. Are you OK?" Jeff examined Jimmy for injuries. There were only one or two peck marks. "I guess you gave as good as you got." Jeff glanced to where he had killed the last zombie turkey that had attacked Sam. It was gone.

* * *

He had no memory of being shot or stabbed. He just awoke with a ravenous hunger in the red snow, stood up, and sniffed the air. Blood. There was the scent of his flock. He followed it. They needed him to lead them. And he needed to feed.

* * *

"Gobble! Gobble!"

"Get into the basement and lock the door!" Phil Sanderson pointed at their stairs. "I'll hold them off up here!" His wife, Dora, ran down carrying their newborn.

Spinning while wielding a kitchen knife and Chinese chopper, Phil knocked one zombie turkey into the blender on the island. The next turkey got its head cut off. Turning back to the one scrambling on the floor, flapping its wings, he hit it in the spine between the wings.

No time to dispatch them permanently. Another turkey flew in the broken window with a cloud of snow. A chopper to the chest and a swipe across the neck put him out of action.

Phil saw dozens of turkeys heading toward his window across the snowy backyard. Desperately he picked up the heavy kitchen island off its rollers and placed it in the sink. Its heavy cutting-board top blocked the broken window.

The turkeys arrived, crashing into the hardwood table. They kept pounding at it, like twenty-pound sledge hammers.

Phil braced it with a hammer and an iron griddle, wedged in the sink against the island's frame. The upper window broke, but the island's tough surface held.

Phil quartered the two turkeys in the kitchen. Everyone knew they had to be split to stop their regeneration, but he figured the smaller pieces, the better. Their heads were already growing back. He piled the pieces into the kitchen sink, further bracing the sturdy island.

"Hmmm. It's cold enough in the kitchen to keep them fresh. Maybe we can eat them later. I hear zombie turkeys are tasty."

The thumps on the island diminished, but he heard pecking elsewhere in the house. Soon, they'd break another window.

"I'd better distract them somehow." Phil ran to his side door. "Hey, turkeys! Come over here!" He sped outside, carrying the chopper and knife. A couple of turkeys peered around the corner of his house and signaled "Gobble! Gobble!"

"I'll gobble you." Phil slogged through the snow to the front of his house. He pressed the keypad on the garage door. Nothing.

Around the corner of the house came a dozen turkeys. He pressed the keypad again, and the door went up.

The turkeys were on him. Phil stabbed one as he squatted and then rolled under the opening door. He chopped off the head of the first one to follow him, sliced the neck of the next, but the third, fourth, and fifth pecked him from the sides.

Bleeding, he backed between the cars. They couldn't fly over the two vans filling the garage, so they had to face his cutlery.

Like avian berserkers, they flew up between the cars, impaling themselves on his knife and chopper. Two turkeys ran below the others and ripped his legs with their spurs. Flinging the bloody turkeys off the kitchen utensils, he brought his blades of death upon the poultry necks.

Four down and bleeding. Not only were there four more behind them, but the whole garage door opening was darkened by the flock. "Well, Phil, you certainly distracted them."

Phil stabbed the first two and left his tools of death in them. He backed farther into the garage and pulled a pick and an axe off the walls. These would give him more reach. His peck wounds bled and hurt despite the cold garage.

Swinging one in each hand, like John Henry hammering railroad spikes, he smashed and crushed his way back between the cars. He incapacitated each turkey with one blow, using short chopping motions so could quickly hit each one.

He kicked the bleeding turkeys ahead of him until he had a wall in front of him. Now they could only attack from above.

And attack they did. Like sharks attracted to chum, they came at him, and Phil turned them into chum. His adrenaline kept him going and going, but after a while noticed he was slowing. He was weary. Despite making heaps of turkeys, they kept coming, like aerial piranhas. The flock of turkeys outside his garage had not diminished, but thickened, darkening the winter morning light. The incessant "Gobble! Gobble!" numbed his ears.

Phil retreated between the cars. He pressed the interior garage door switch. The door started closing but reopened when it hit the mound of turkeys. *Damn safety feature.*

Worst of all, the first turkeys he'd killed were stirring. Severed heads had grown back. Split chests and backs were healed. "Gobble? Gobble?" they said as they stood uncertainly.

He squared his shoulders. He'd go down in a blaze of glory.

* * *

After leaving Sam with the medic, Jeff crawled back into the MRAP with Jimmy.

"OK, we need to proceed to Fairview Acres immediately," Lieutenant Avery said. "Several motorists are stranded there."

"Stuck in the snow?" Jeff opened his overalls as the MRAP jolted down the road.

"It's not clear. The drivers are surrounded by turkeys and can't move. It's a report from one of our copters. We'll see soon."

They turned down Fairview Road and saw hundreds of turkeys besieging two cars. They appeared mired in red mud.

"Specialist Jones, flame on either side of those cars. Let's put them on the run."

Gouts of napalm flooded the ground near the cars. Turkeys roasted before their eyes. The scent of Thanksgiving dinner came through the ventilation system.

Turkeys outside the walls of flame scattered into the woods. Those between continued attacking the car. A windshield shattered.

"Gunners! Pick off those turkeys on the cars ASAP! Sergeant Swanson, you go out too," Lieutenant Avery ordered.

Jeff knelt in the snow and sighted. One turkey on the hood presented its profile, fifty yards away. Crack! The turkey flopped off the hood with a center body-mass hit.

On to the next. Beside him, Privates Hurley and Jimenez fired in one- and two-bullet bursts.

"The great Cearfoss turkey shoot." Jimenez reloaded his M4. "Thirty rounds go quickly when you're having fun."

"Shut up and shoot," Hurley growled as he reloaded his weapon.

"Just a few more on the cars." Jeff jammed in a fresh magazine as well.

"Now we get to go full auto." Jimenez fired into the crowd between the cars. Some flew up between the flames, where Hurley picked them off. Others flew into the flames, bursting into fire and falling among the other roasting poultry.

The rest flew directly toward them. The hunting team fired full auto at them, but they were less accurate. The zombie turkeys were ten yards away when a new voice was heard. Out of the secondary firing port in the MRAP, the fléchette gun fired. On full automatic. Each .50 shell separated into four fléchettes. Each contained salt water. Forty rounds fired in the first six seconds. The oncoming flock exploded into shredded turkeys.

Jeff and the other gunners flinched as a cloud of blood droplets showered on them.

"Hey, Fred! Did you have to wait until the last second?" Hurley groused.

"Cleanup on aisle Fairview Road." Jimenez grinned at Jeff.

"Lieutenant Avery here. Well done, men. As you know, Private Hurley, the fléchettes are most effective at short range. Specialist Zagrev fired on my order."

"Yes, sir."

"Now check on the motorists. See if they need medical attention."

"Yes, sir."

Jeff walked to the cars, their engines still running. The ground turkeys made red mud. It reddened his boots.

Both cars had shattered windshields, one with a fist-sized hole. A woman rested with her head on the steering wheel. She looked up at them and rolled down the window. Tears streaked her face.

"You saved us. Thank you."

"Are you OK, ma'am?" Hurley asked.

"Yes. They didn't get in. I just need a hot coffee—with some Irish whiskey."

"Yes, ma'am. We'll see what we can do."

Jimenez listened to the other driver. "We slammed into this flock on the road at sixty, seventy miles per hour. A turkey broke my windshield. We tried to drive through them, but they followed us, pecking all the way. Then turkey guts spewed all over the road, and we lost traction. We rocked back and forth, but there were always more turkeys. I thought we were goners."

"That's my husband, Terry. I'm Frida. We're the Calloways. He and I left at the same time this morning. He was going to work in Hagerstown, and I was taking our kids to preschool. We live in Fairview Acres."

"Are you sure you don't need any help? Or your children?" Private Jimenez asked.

"No, just get us out of this mess," Terry said from his car.

"No problem." Hurley turned back to the MRAP. "Hey, Fred! Back up here and tow these cars out."

The six-wheeled MRAP backed to the cars. The soldiers hooked the towing cable to the bumpers and pulled the vehicles free of the pile of poultry parts.

Mr. and Mrs. Calloway drove away in their bloody cars.

Back in the MRAP, the flamethrower cleaned up the mess of bodies. "Men, get in the MRAP." Lieutenant Avery ordered as they watched the flames. "We must proceed immediately to Cearfoss Pike. There's a homeowner in danger there. Fred, here are the GPS coordinates."

They climbed into the MRAP. "Our copter noticed a flock of turkeys around a house and strafed them, but some are still clustered too close to strafe. Fred, go at top speed."

"Yes, sir."

Jeff turned to Lieutenant Avery. He was listening to his comm and making notes on his pad. "When can Jimmy and I get back on turkey patrol?"

"The battle situation is still fluid. I'm still getting reports of pockets of turkey resistance all over the western suburbs. Also, I want to check on Sam Melvin for his advice. We've found some turkeys, but not the main flock yet. I'll let you know."

"There are a few turkeys up ahead," Fred called out. Some turkeys crossed the road ahead.

"Why did the zombie turkey cross the road?" Private Jimenez asked.

"To get to the other side?" Jeff suggested.

"To get something to eat." Jimenez snickered.

"Specialist Zagreb, stop at that house on the right, a hundred yards ahead." Lieutenant Avery pointed at it.

"Yes, sir."

Several hundred turkeys clotted the opening of a double garage of a brick ranch.

"Jimenez, Hurley, Swanson, deploy to the left flank of the turkeys and hit them with enfilading fire on those trying to escape. Swanson, you fire. Zagreb, you pull into the driveway on their right and hit them with fléchettes." He quickly sketched the deployment on his laptop.

"Yes, sir." Jeff, Jimenez, and Hurley hopped out when their driver parked. Fred Zagreb moved to the auxiliary weapons port and prepared the fléchette gun.

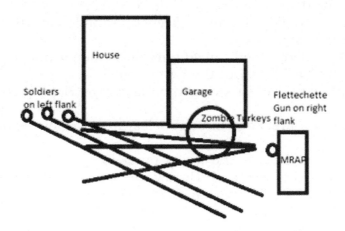

Jeff trotted behind the other soldiers, giving the mob of turkeys wide berth. Surprisingly, they didn't even pay attention. They were cramming into the garage, trying to reach something. Must be some food stored there.

Jeff noticed the turkeys funneled between two vans. A lot of the turkeys had red, bloody marks on their backs and necks. Some were even missing feathers, although they quickly grew back. On impulse, he yelled, "Hey! Anyone in there?"

"Yeah! Hurry up! They just about got me," a man cried from inside.

"We're on it! In a few minutes they'll be gone!" Jimenez yelled as they knelt around the corner of the garage.

"Lieutenant, we're ready," Jeff commed.

"Fire."

The three soldiers shot at the back half of the flock. The rata-tat-tat of the fléchette machine gun drowned out the crackle of their rifles. As the fléchettes turned the flock into a bloody pulp, turkeys flew out of the garage. The three marksmen shot them down.

Jimenez cackled. "Pull! There goes another one. Are you keeping score, Jeff?"

"I'm just trying to get the farthest ones I see."

"Shut up and shoot." Hurley fired as a brace of turkeys flew out the door. Even as he shot, a BRATT! spoke from the machine gun and half a dozen fléchette rounds tore the birds into smithereens.

Click. Jeff reloaded quickly, as did Jimenez and Hurley. They looked for birds, but there were none.

"Lieutenant, we're moving into the garage. Hold fire on the fléchette."

"Hold your fire, Zagreb. You're clear to move now, Sergeant Swanson."

Jeff waded through the turkey muck in front of the garage, followed by Jimenez and Hurley. Inside, he found some bleeding turkeys still breathing. The floor was wet and crusted with turkey blood. No one was visible.

"Anyone here? Cover me. I'm going in." Jeff kicked the bleeding turkeys out of his way as he worked his way between the vans.

Around the front he found a bloodied man sitting against the door with a cleaver in one hand and a foot-long kitchen knife in the other. Checking his pulse, Jeff found he was still alive—barely.

"Men, quarter those turkeys. Lieutenant Avery, we need medics here ASAP."

"Sergeant, I've already called in a medivac copter. After we've stopped the remaining turkeys from resurrecting, we'll return to the medic truck to check on our zombie detective."

When the crew returned to the MRAP, the lieutenant turned to them. "Men, the turkeys have fled back to the woods and rivers. The helicopters are harassing the flocks from the air. This mission is completed."

Back at the Cearfoss intersection, the medical lieutenant came to meet Lieutenant Avery.

"Mike! I'm glad you're here. I've got a stubborn civilian who refuses to go to the hospital. He says he's militarily necessary. He agreed to do whatever you say."

"Thanks for the background, Scott. Let's see our civilian."

Sam sat in the MRAP in his shirt, no longer connected to the IV. He leaned forward, obviously avoiding pressing against his heavily bandaged back.

"We've defeated the turkeys, Sam. They've retreated into the woods. Thank you for your invaluable help," Lieutenant Avery said.

"Probably not, Lieutenant. The main flock is hibernating and healing, I'd bet."

"Still, our aerial estimates are that at least half the flock, over twenty-five thousand turkeys, is permanently eliminated.

"They'll be back in four weeks. zombie turkeys reproduce and grow faster than normal turkeys. They'll double their population in that time, given enough food."

"Then what should we do?"

"Devote all your soldiers to finding the hibernating turkeys. Keep going along every creek and river. Hire hunting dogs and expand your K-9 corps. Finally, call in all the hunters from out of state. There seems to be a break in the weather."

"Lieutenant Weatherby said you refused to go to the hospital. Why?"

"I'm fine, just a little tender. You need me, the captain needs me, and the governor of the state of Maryland needs me."

"I love your dedication, Sam. Let's go talk with the captain. I'll give my report, and you can give yours. Private Zagreb, take us to headquarters."

On the way, Lisa called Sam.

"Hi, Sam. How are you doing?"

"OK, I guess. I got pecked by zombie turkeys, but they patched me up. In my parka, I can lean against the seat without much pain."

"So you found them! Good job. I heard about the victory over the zombie turkeys in Hagerstown. You're a hero! I'm proud of you. Can you type up a report for the *Midley Beacon*? We'll pay you commission, your usual daily salary."

"That's great, Lisa! Does this mean I'm back full time at the *Beacon*?"

"Nope. Sorry. We're still not making enough subscription and ad revenue. But we can report about your success as a zombie detective, including your phone number and email.

That'll get you more business. We won't even charge you for advertising."

"What a deal."

"I'd better let you go. You sound tired. Bye, Sam."

"Bye, Lisa," Sam said to the silent phone. As usual, Lisa had hung up after "Bye, Sam."

After they stopped at the National Guard headquarters, Lieutenant Avery gave his report to Captain Carpenter.

The captain turned and said, "Sam? Is there anything you'd like to add?"

"Yes. Now is the time to strike the hibernating turkeys hard. Use all your troops to seek them out along the creeks and rivers around the Potomac. Maybe enlist private hunters as well."

"We'll certainly do that. But getting the hunters back is above my pay grade. As you saw, we've lost some to these turkeys."

"Hmmm. I wonder if the governor would make a plea for hunters to return to Maryland? Let me give her a call." Sam slid his cell from his pocket.

"You have her on speed dial?"

"Yup. I called her on the way into Maryland." Sam punched the "Governor Mary Landis" number.

"Hello, Governor Landis. I'm here with Captain Carpenter. Let me put you on speakerphone."

"Hello, Governor."

"Hello, Captain. I'm hearing good things about the battle today."

"Yes. We estimate the turkey casualties at over twenty thousand. That's permanently dead, quartered and burned."

"The reason we called, Governor Landis, is we need your help," Sam said. "The military will do the best they can at finding the hibernating turkeys, but what you really need are turkey hunters. If you make a public appeal for them to return, each one will help."

"I'll do that at my news conference tonight. Captain, email me a briefing. I'll see what I can do to waive hunting fees for the period of this emergency."

"That's great!"

"Sam, we've really made progress since you've been here. Can we call you if the problem ever rears its turkey head again?"

"Yes, ma'am. I'm at your disposal."

"Go ahead and head home to Illinois. Your work here is done."

* * *

Lisa met Sam at the Peoria airport that evening, running through the lobby and jump-hugging him. "Sam! I'm glad you're home."

"Ow! Watch it, Lisa. My back is still sore."

"Oh. Sorry. The good news is, your check from Maryland arrived. Your detective agency turned a profit."

"Great!"

"More good news—your account of the battle of Cearfoss Maryland sold out this edition of the *Midley Beacon*. Finally, your dashcam video from your Hunt Master went viral on YouTube! We haven't had a viral video for almost two months."

"All this goodness almost makes me forget my tender back."

"How about a steak dinner at the best restaurant in Peoria?"

"That will do it. Nothing like a rare steak to soothe zombie turkey bites."

Chapter 5 - Down on the Farm

"Bye, Sam. I'm off to work." She smooched him. Lisa was leaving late, at seven instead of six.

"Bye, Lisa. I can hardly wait to see the effect of the *Midley Beacon* mentioning my detective agency."

"See you at the office after I finish breakfast."

Sam gasped as he opened his email. Over fourteen hundred in his inbox! He sorted them by the sender and deleted or moved about half of them.

His cell phone rang.

"Hello, Sam Melvin, zombie detective."

"Hi, Sam, this is Betty Williams, formerly Betty Tuffield of Henry. Do you remember me?"

"Of course, Betty! Congratulations on your wedding! Sorry Lisa and I couldn't come. President Obama invited us to the White House for New Year's Eve."

"That's OK. We just had a private wedding, Hank and I, just before the new year. But I called you with a problem I hope you can solve."

"What's that?"

"We have a zombie turkey problem."

"Oh no, I still am healing from my last zombie turkey problem!"

"Yes, I read about Hagerstown in the *Midley Beacon*. How bad was it?"

"Pretty bad. People were killed and injured. Not as bad as last Thanksgiving's zombie turkey apocalypse, of course."

"Yep, that was one for the history books. Our problem is smaller. We have zombie turkeys escaping, and we don't know where or how."

"That could be bad."

"Nah. We've caught most of them with Tom Tuffield's Zombie Turkey Traps. We adapted them for live catching."

"So what do you need me for?"

"To think like a turkey! Figure out how they're escaping so we can stop them."

"You sure you can afford my standard rates?"

"I saw them on your website. We're actually doing pretty well. I'll tell you more when you get here."

"See you in a couple of hours!"

* * *

Sam beat his two-hour estimate on the way to the Tuffield farm in Henry, Illinois. When Hank Williams and Betty Tuffield had married the previous year, they'd merged their farms and turkey businesses. Betty had already converted her farm into making zombie turkey sausage. She collected the thousands of turkey corpses ground, squished, or split into non-resurrecting meat and sold them as a novelty item on the internet (not for human consumption). Later, since so many people were buying her zombie sausages and eating them, she started raising zombie turkeys for meat.

Hank Williams (named after the singer) had restocked his farm with regular turkeys after the zombie turkey apocalypse. The couple kept the two farms going, one for zombies, one for regular turkeys. They lived at Hank's homestead west of Maneno, Illinois, so his three children could continue to attend their schools, but traveled almost every day to Henry.

Betty and Hank greeted him as he pulled in front of the barn.

"Hi, Sam!" Betty's smile lit up her square face, framed by auburn hair.

"Welcome to Tuffields' Turkeys, the foremost purveyor of zombie turkey sausage, legs, and wings." Hank sounded proud. Hank was a tall dark-haired man with broad shoulders and a craggy face.

"Whoa! You've really expanded here Hank, Betty."

"Yes, we've had one hundred percent monthly growth since Thanksgiving." Now Betty sounded proud.

"But the zombie turkeys are eating into our profits."

"So show me your operation. I recognize your original barn. I can see the Tuffield Traps around it, but there have been a lot of changes."

"After I lost Tom and the turkey flock, I started making zombie turkey sausage, mostly for revenge," Betty said.

"I could understand that, having lost my wife, Laura, to the turkeys." Hank looked at Betty.

"I kept the zombie turkeys in steel cages. We'd sometimes find one or two alive in our zombie-killing traps."

"I remember those," Sam said. "You had one with swinging chainsaws and a couple with wood chippers. They're still selling on the *Midley Beacon* website."

"Those sales are steady income, but zombie turkeys are our bread and butter. Or sausage, legs, and wings."

"So show me your new stuff. How do you kill them for wings and legs? Don't you sell the breast meat too?"

"It's easier to show you than to tell." Hank led them to a building adjacent to the barn. A three-foot-square steel chain-link tunnel led to the building. It was filled with zombie turkeys.

"Gobble! Gobble!"

"I'm going to have to shout to be heard over them!" Hank opened the door.

The turkeys came out of a revolving door, one at a time. A side of beef hung in the room in front of the door. One turkey rushed and attacked it. Clamps came up from the floor and down from the ceiling and grabbed the bird by its chest. Circular saw blades attached to the upper and lower clamps cut off the turkey's wings and legs. The zombie quadruple amputee fell onto a conveyer belt below the floor, which took the bird back to the barn.

The door rotated, and the next bird came out. The wings and the legs fells into separate bins.

"Wow. I get it! Just losing their wings and legs isn't enough to kill them. They grow them back. How long does that take?"

"Only about an hour. When we're done harvesting wings and legs from the whole flock, we start over again," Hank said.

"It was Hank's idea."

"But you helped with the mechanics of it."

"You learn a little mechanics after ten years as a farmer's wife."

"So where does your famous zombie turkey sausage come from?"

"We're still going through freezer loads of birds from Thanksgiving." Betty gestured toward another building.

Sam could hear a wood chipper inside it.

"We had an attack by thousands of birds on Thanksgiving Day. We collected a lot then." Hank looked at Betty. She continued.

"Then when the zombie turkey plague broke out all over the country after Thanksgiving, we bought all the dead turkeys we could."

"Nobody wanted them. We made a killing." Hank kept a straight face.

"Of course, we had to buy a couple of big commercial freezers."

"Room sized. Betty got them at a discount. She can squeeze a penny until it screams."

"A lot of turkey farmers went out of business. They were glad to sell them."

"Do you want to see the sausage making, Sam?"

"No, Hank. I believe the old saying, 'You never want to see sausage being made.'"

"Oh c'mon," Betty said. "You've seen gorier things than that, covering the turkey apocalypse."

"Yeah, I have, but that doesn't mean I have to like it. But I should see it, to see if there's a place for the turkeys to escape."

Betty stared at him. "Um, frozen turkeys don't escape."

"Oh, right. So the only place is this wing and leg building and the barn?" Sam looked at Hank.

"Yup. And we've been over every inch of the tunnel and barn, looking for escape routes."

"Including the roof?"

"Definitely. That's how the zombies got in originally and killed poor Tom." Betty shivered.

"I remember. OK, how about underground?"

"What?" They stared at him blankly.

"You know, when zombie turkeys feed in the wild, they dig underground and hibernate for a couple of days. Have you seen them digging in your barn?"

"Uh, no. I've noticed they go to sleep in their cages after feeding, but I never looked for tunnels. I didn't know that." Hank looked sheepish, for a turkey farmer.

"That's what we'll do today."

They entered the big barn. It held perhaps six hundred turkeys. "Gobble! Gobble!" Twelve hundred red eyes looked at Sam.

"That sound still gives me the creeps."

"You get used to it. Where do we start?"

"Hank, we've got to look under every cage."

"We'll start with the one we've emptied for leg and wing processing. The turkeys are dumped back in the big cage, and then we separate them."

"If we don't, the toms fight each other to death," Betty added.

"I'll bet they come back to life." Sam looked at her.

"Yup. And then they fight again. It's a real bother."

The holding pen was about twenty feet square. It led to the processing tunnel. Sam could hear "Gobble! Gobble" coming from there. He was glad to see a one-way spring door that could be pushed open by the turkeys from the pen but not from the tunnel.

He wasn't so glad about the stench of turkey droppings. He wrinkled his nose.

"Yeah, it gets a bit ripe in here," Betty said. "The dung bin is due for spreading on the fields, Hank."

"Yeah, I nose."

"Ha."

They examined the floor carefully. Nothing, just hard-packed dirt and straw.

"Where next, zombie detective?"

Sam eyed the cages surrounding the barn. Half were on the floor, and half were above them. "How many cages do you have on the floor?"

"About three hundred. Another four hundred are on a second tier. We're planning a third tier," Hank said.

"OK. We'll split up. I'll go left, Hank will go right, and Betty, you go straight and work your way back toward us."

"Sounds good."

Sam scanned each cage as he moved to the back of the barn. He studied the ground and checked the steel cages for breaks. Some birds charged at the bars until they knocked themselves out. Some gobbled at him. But all of them eyed him with their red glowing eyes.

"Hey! I've found something!" Betty called from the corner cage ahead of Sam.

Sam and Hank ran to her. She pointed at a mound of dirt in the farthest corner. "That looks like a tunnel."

"Or at least a hole. Can you move the turkeys out of here? Safely?"

"Of course! We're professional zombie turkey farmers." Hank felt in his coat pockets, then looked at Betty. "Do you have any?"

"Don't leave home without it." Betty smiled and looked at Sam. "Watch this."

She took a plastic bag out of her pocket, filled with a pink mass. She took out a pinch, formed a ball, and held it in front of the turkeys. "Go get it, boys and girls." She opened the cage door and threw the wad into the holding pen in the middle of the barn.

Six zombie turkeys ran out of the cage for the holding pen. They ran through a one-way door in the pen. The first one gobbled the ball. The late ones looked around, pecking the ground.

"That sure worked. What is that stuff?"

"Ground hamburger. It works better than anything for getting their attention. It's sort of like an MRE for zombie turkeys," Hank said.

"That answers my question about how you get the turkeys into the holding pen."

"They're really quite predictable. Show them raw meat, and they'll go after it." Hank held the door open for them as they entered.

The mound of dirt didn't seem to be a tunnel. Hank dug down using a shovel, and they found five eggs.

"Huh. Do you collect turkey eggs?"

"Some, but we've been encouraging them to breed to increase our flock. All our breeders were supposed to be on the second level. These turkeys are too young to breed."

"Uh, no. Dr. Galloway of the Turkey Institute found out they breed faster and come to maturity sooner than regular turkeys."

"I knew they were nearly fully grown in three weeks, but these poults are six weeks old."

"There doesn't seem to be a tunnel here, but can you dig along the wall, Hank?"

"Sure." Hank obliged. Along the back wall of the barn, the shovel broke through into an underground cavity.

"Oho! Let's take a look at this." Sam peered into the hole as Hank expanded it. "It's right next to the cornerstone of the barn."

"What?" Betty asked.

"The tunnel leading out. The turkeys covered it up when they laid their eggs."

"You'd almost think they had intelligence and were planning a breakout."

"The Great Escape of zombie turkeys. Could be a movie," Hank said. "I'll pour a couple of bags of concrete into the tunnel and put a steel grate in the gap in the foundation."

"Are there any other gaps?" Sam asked.

"Yeah, in the other corners of the barn, next to each cornerstone."

"Let's check those cages too."

"We've already checked the ones by the front of the barn."

"I haven't checked the other back corner," Betty said.

They found no other tunnels.

"Whew! That could have been worse." Hank poured bags of concrete into the hole and then soaked it with a hose.

"Thanks, Sam. What do we owe you?" Betty brought out her checkbook.

"Uh, a thousand is my daily rate. But make it just five hundred. You're my friends."

"Thanks, Sam. But you're our friend too, and you've saved us thousands. Here's your check."

* * *

Back at his home in Midley, Sam came in after Lisa, for a change.

"My zombie detective!" Lisa threw herself at him and kissed him. "Whew! You stink of zombie turkeys. I know that smell well. Go shower."

"Then we can renew kissing?"

"Nah. I'll come and scrub your back for you."

"I love marriage."

Chapter 6 – The Carnivore Diet

The sound of "Over the River and through the Woods" played on Sam's phone and tablet early the next morning.

"What's that, Sam?" Lisa said.

"Oh, I picked that as my ring tone for my business. It reminds me of Thanksgiving, which reminds me of the zombie turkeys. Hello? Sam Melvin, zombie detective." Sam picked up the tablet and activated the camera.

"Oh, Mr. Melvin, I hope you can help me. I'm Doris Franklin, from Keokuk, Iowa. I've got a terrible problem. My husband has started eating raw meat."

"Uh, marriage counseling is not really in my line of work. That seems like a personal choice. Have you talked with him?"

"Yes, I warned him he'd get sick, but he swears he's never felt better!"

"Why did you call me, Mrs. Franklin? I'm a detective, not a psychologist or counselor."

"I think he's turning into a zombie! He likes raw brains!"

"Cow brains, I hope."

"Well, yes. We raise cattle here."

"Unless his eyes turn red, he's not a zombie."

"No, his eyes are gorgeous blue, just like they were when I married him."

"Then I can say with certainty he's not a zombie."

"How many human zombies have you met?"

"Uh, none. Just turkeys, squirrels, and cows."

"Then how do you know human's eyes turn red?"

"I guess I don't."

"Then come here and see what you can do."

"I hate to waste your money."

Doris knelt in front of the camera. She clasped her hands imploringly. "But, Sam Melvin! You're my only hope! I really can't take this to anyone else I'd trust to keep it quiet. You are a licensed private eye, right?"

"Right."

"See, I'll pay in advance on your website. Now you have to come."

"OK. I'll see what I can do to help your husband. Let's see how far Keokuk is from Midley." Sam looked up the distance on the internet. "It's about a hundred and forty miles by car, but only ninety-five by air. Let's see if I can fly there."

"We're not a big city like Des Moines or Peoria. I don't think you can get a flight."

"We have a private plane. Let's see about the nearest airport to Keokuk." Consulting the trusty internet again, Sam found the Keokuk Municipal Airport. "OK, I can get there in less than two hours. I'll have to call our pilot and set it up. Can you give me your address?"

"Sure. We're right outside Argyle on Route 29. We're called 'Beefy Farm.' Rural Route 37. You can't miss it."

"'You can't miss it' is a sure sign I will. I'll use GPS."

"I'm not sure that works out here."

"I'll do my best, Mrs. Franklin. Look for me within two hours."

"Thanks, Sam. Bye."

"Bye."

Sam called Dan Cosana, their pilot. They met at the Peoria airport half an hour later.

"Private aviation is so much more convenient than commercial." Sam settled into the passenger seat of the *Midley Beacon*'s Turbo Arrow.

"I'd rather fly myself than take commercial, even if it takes twice as long." Dan took off.

Sam loved watching the airspeed climb from ninety at takeoff to one hundred forty as they climbed.

"That's always a rush. What's our ETA, Dan?"

"Looks like ten o'clock, at a hundred and seventy knots."

"That'll give me half an hour to get to Beefy Farms. I'll be right on time."

* * *

After picking up his rental car at Keokuk airport, Sam drove past cows grazing on fields of green and brown with patches of snow. A hand-painted sign read "Beefy Farms: 100% All-Natural Grass-Fed Beef" and showed a smiling cow. Sam pulled into the driveway of the farmhouse, got out, and knocked on the door.

A middle-aged lady with short brown hair answered the door.

"Hi. You must be Sam Melvin. You look just like you did on the video call."

"I guess so. You must be Mrs. Franklin."

"Call me Doris. My husband is Bryan."

"Where is Bryan?"

"He's out working in the barn."

"OK. Mind if I go see him?"

"No, he's expecting you."

The warm, earthy smell of cows greeted Sam in the barn. Bryan was squatting on a concrete pad, working on the milk pump.

"Hi, I'm Sam Melvin, zombie detective."

Bryan stood, tall and angular, brushed his hands off on his pants, and shook Sam's hand. "Hi, Sam. My wife called you to help with my meat craving."

"I warned her I wasn't sure I'd help. But I do have a lot of experience with zombies. But you're obviously not." Sam nodded at him as he looked into his bright-blue eyes. "So when did this carnivore diet start?"

"Just after the first of the year. Vegetables and even bread lost their appeal, and meat became so much tastier. Especially raw."

"Did you go raw all at once?"

"Nah. I ate my steak rarer and rarer, until one day I just microwaved my hamburger to body temperature. It was delicious. I haven't gone back."

"OK." Sam typed notes into his tablet. "Any other changes you've noticed?"

"I've never felt so good in my life! The cold weather doesn't bother me much, and I have so much energy. I've gotten to chores I always put off, like maintaining this milk pump." Bryan gestured to the motor.

"That sounds cool."

"I'm just about done here." Bryan closed the cover on the pump, picked it up onto a dolly, and wheeled it into the pump room.

"You're pretty strong. What does that pump weigh? It must be over a hundred pounds."

"Yup. I'm stronger than I look. I've worked with cows since I was a kid."

"So this is a dairy farm?"

"And I raise beef too. It works out well. I sell the cows I can't milk, and milk the ones I can." Bryan walked by a stall. "Here's Bessie. She's one of our best milkers." He patted her rump fondly.

Bessie kicked Bryan in the leg, knocking him down. Then she turned her head and looked at him.

"Ooh, that smarts." Bryan rubbed his shin.

"Should I call a doctor?" Sam grabbed his phone from his jeans pocket.

"Nah, I'll be fine in a moment. Ugh. I got something in my eye. I gotta change my contact."

"I gotta go to the restroom too."

"It's over here." Bryan led the way, with one eye closed, limping slightly.

Bryan washed his hands, took out his contact, and washed it in the sink. Sam, washing his hands in the other sink, glanced at Bryan's reflection. Bryan had one bright-blue eye and one glowing red eye.

"Bryan! You're a zombie!"

"Nah, what are you talking about? My eye's just irritated from something."

Sam peered closer at his eye. "No, it's definitely glowing, reflecting light. That's a sign of zombie animals. They grow a layer of blood cells that amplify light and improve night vision."

"You sure it isn't conjunctivitis? Pink eye?" Bryan frowned at his reflection.

"Positive. I've had that, and it looks nothing like it. But it looks just like the thousands of zombies I've seen."

"Let's see what Doris thinks. She's my amateur doctor." They went back to the house.

"Doris! Come look at this."

"What happened to your eye?" She ran to Bryan and peered at his eye.

"It's been red for a couple of weeks now. I thought it was just pink eye."

"You should have stopped wearing your contacts! They can carry the infection. Get rid of them right now."

"OK. But Sam here thinks it's a sign I'm a zombie."

"Oh, I didn't think of that." She looked even closer at his eye. "It doesn't look irritated. It looks like it's glowing. Is the other one like that?"

"It was this morning when I put the contacts in." Bryan popped out the other contact and pitched it into the wastebasket.

Doris looked at him and winced. "All right. I think this means you're a zombie."

"I can't believe it!"

"There's a surefire test. Turn off the lights in the room and cover the windows. Your eyes will glow with any remaining light," Sam said.

"OK. Let's go to the billiard room. That has no windows." They went into the Franklins' finished basement.

"Huh. You're the first person I know with a billiard room. I thought that was just in Clue," Sam said.

"We went to England on our honeymoon, and we both learned to love billiards," Doris said.

Bryan closed the door. "Here goes!" He turned out the lights.

Two red eyes glowed where Bryan stood.

"You're a zombie all right. You could get hired as a stoplight."

"Uh-oh. I've never heard of a human turning zombie before."

"Me neither. I knew about the turkeys, of course, and the stories about squirrels and cows I read in the *Midley Beacon*. Why did it have to be Bryan?" Doris burst into tears. She wiped her eyes and sighed. "I guess I kind of feared this ever since you started eating raw meat. But it's funny—now that I know, I feel more at ease. Now that I know he's a zombie, I can accept his diet."

"There, there, Mrs. Franklin, I'm sure he can be cured."

"He can?"

"Of course. We dezombify turkeys all the time with salt water."

"Oh, I guess I knew that. Bryan even has a saltwater tank set up in case any of our cattle turn zombie."

"Doris, I'm sorry. I don't know how this happened."

"Maybe I do," Sam said.

"What do you mean?" Bryan turned the lights back on and looked at Sam redly.

"Lisa and I investigated the source of the zombie turkey outbreak. It was a side effect of Corn-All's GMO modified corn on turkey gut bacteria. Each of the other zombie animals also ate that corn. Do you have any Corn-All grain?"

"Nah. I use another brand for my cows, plus hay and pasturage." Bryan frowned.

"Uh, Bryan, don't you like grits for breakfast?" Doris raised an eyebrow.

"Sure, that's my favorite."

"I think that's made by Corn-All."

"Let's see the box," Sam said.

Doris led them upstairs to their kitchen. "Here it is. See, it says 'Made from all-natural corn grown in America's heartland. Made by Mighty Bites Cereal company, a wholly owned subsidiary of Corn-All.'"

"That just about clinches it. What's the expiration date on the box?"

"I just bought it. Two weeks from now."

"So it's been made since Thanksgiving. That's when Lisa and I investigated Corn-All and found their zombie connection. But they said they destroyed all their GMO grain."

"I guess they didn't," Bryan said. "Now what?"

"We can try salt water like we did with zombie turkeys. Spraying them with salt water kills their zombie bacteria."

"I installed a salt sprayer in my barn when I found out about the zombie plague. I didn't want my cows catching it."

"Are you willing to try it?"

"Sure. Let's go. I could use a bath."

Back out they tromped to the barn. "This'll be the first time I tried it on myself. Do I need to take off my clothing?" Bryan stood in the shower room, near the barn entrance, holding the pull rope.

"I don't think so. None of the turkeys took off their feathers, and it worked on them."

"Here goes!" He pulled the rope and thoroughly drenched himself. "Did it work?" He looked at them.

"Nope. Maybe it doesn't work on humans. Too bad you don't have a hypodermic needle. You could try an injection of it."

"Of course I have a hypodermic needle, several of them, for my cows. I vaccinate them myself." Bryan dripped over to his office in the barn and retrieved a medical kit with a large needle. He started filling it with saltwater.

"I'd better get some medical advice." Sam punched his phone.

"Who are you calling, Sam?" Doris asked.

"Dr. Ed Galloway of the Turkey Institute. He helped us with the zombie turkeys. Maybe he can help with zombie people."

"Good idea. Bryan, hold off on the injection until we know what's what."

"Why, Doris? I've used it hundreds of times on my cows. Salt water is harmless. What have I got to lose?"

"Just wait, for my sake."

"OK."

"Hi, Dr. Galloway. This is Sam Melvin. How are you? . . . Good. Well, I've got a zombie question, but this is about zombie humans. Would it be safe to inject a zombie human with salt water? We've already tried a saltwater spray. Would an injection help?" Sam listened to the answer for a long time.

"OK, let me get that number. I'll tell the Franklins. They're the couple whose husband has turned zombie. . . . Thanks. Goodbye."

"What's the word?" Bryan's red eyes bored into Sam's.

"Dr. Galloway isn't sure if it'll work, especially since the saltwater spray failed. He agrees it wouldn't hurt to try it, as long as your needle is clean."

"Of course. I disinfect before and after each injection, even between cows."

"OK. Dr. Galloway has a contact in the Mayo Clinic, Dr. Herbst, who wants to study your blood. Could you take a sample of your blood before you take the salt water? I'll send it to her."

"Sure. What's a little bit of blood for medical science? Who knows—it might be able to help someone. Doris, will you do the honors?"

"Of course, Bryan." Doris held up a vial, attached a sterile needle, and drew blood from Bryan's arm.

Sam looked away. "Sorry. I get squeamish at the sight of blood."

Doris laughed. "You'd never be able to do my job. I'm a hematologist. I take blood samples of the cows and people. That's how I worked my way through college." She finished up, dropped the needle into a jar of alcohol, sealed the vial, and handed it to Sam. "I hope that doesn't make you queasy!" She smiled.

"I just pretend it's red paint."

"OK, it's my turn to man the needle." Bryan took the syringe full of salt water and carefully injected it into the same vein Doris had used.

"Isn't that sore?" Doris asked.

"Nope. I recover real fast from little pokes and jabs. Even getting kicked by Bessie only knocked me down."

"You know she kicks. Why weren't you careful?"

"I wasn't milking her, so I didn't expect it. OK. That's that. Tell me what you see."

"Hmmm. With zombie turkeys, it takes less than a minute when the army hits them with saltwater fléchettes. You're bigger than a turkey, so it might take longer."

"I think your eyes don't look as red." Doris watched him carefully.

"I don't feel any different."

"I think Doris is right. Your eyes look kind of reddish-brown now."

"My eyes have never been brown before. Just blue."

"Until they turned red. Brown eyes look good on you, Bryan. I would never have guessed." Doris peered deeper into his eyes.

"Will they turn blue again, Sam?"

"How would I know? I'm no doctor. But zombie turkeys eyes turn black like normal after salt water."

"Your eyes are lightening. They look kind of hazel now," Doris said.

"You get three men in a day for the price of one: red eyed, brown eyed, and now hazel."

"And soon blue. They really are changing fast. That's what, five minutes?"

"Now I've got my blue-eyed husband back! All thanks, to you Sam!"

"Me—and salt water."

Chapter 7 – Interview

"Sam, that was a great story you sent me. I already sent your payment electronically."

"Thanks, Lisa! That's almost as good as the kiss you gave me when I came home."

"You mushball! That's one of the reasons I love you. You don't really care about money at all, do you?"

"Not really. I'd rather have friends."

"Well, you got me as your friend, and I'm a tough nut to crack. I probably started liking you four or five years after we worked together."

"I never knew. I always liked you, since high school."

"Yeah, well, to me you were just another dumb guy then. Now you're my only guy." She hugged him.

"Mmm. S'nice. Now you're turning into a mushball."

"Let's do something about that before you get another phone call or email."

And so to bed, before dinner.

* * *

As Lisa predicted, Sam soon received emails, hundreds of them, from his article about the "Zombie Cow Farmer" (Lisa's title). But it was a phone call that came as he brushed his teeth that evening that caught his attention.

"Mmmf! Splat! Hello?"

"Hi, Sam. This is Oprah. Oprah Winfrey."

"Oh, hi, Oprah! You surprised me. I was just getting ready for bed."

"Seven thirty? Oh, it's nine thirty there in the Midwest. Are you an early-to-bed, early-to-rise guy?"

"Well, kind of."

"Anyway, I loved your article in the *Midley Beacon*, about the zombie cow farmer."

"That was fast! Lisa just published it this evening."

"Oh, I get notified whenever the *Midley Beacon* publishes anything on the web. Anyway, it was a revelation that humans can get the zombie disease, like turkeys."

"And squirrels. And cows. And who knows what else. So how are things with you? I haven't heard from you since we won the lifetime supply of turkeys from you. We're still enjoying them, by the way."

"I'm glad to hear that. I called you, Sam, in your professional capacity as a zombie detective. I've already advanced you a week's pay."

"Uh, normally I talk to you before you pay."

"This is for your special zombie expertise. I'd like to find another zombie human, like the man in your story."

"OK, but I can't guarantee you success."

"I'm sure you'll succeed. I'll just keep paying you until you do!"

"I suppose that's one way to do it. But why? Why do you want a zombie person? To interview on your show?"

"Why . . . yes! Er, that's it! You guessed it."

"I'll do my best."

"I'm sure you will. Just call me at this number each day and tell me your progress."

"OK, will do."

"Great! See you later, you zombie detective."

Lisa stared at him as he set the phone down.

"Did I hear you that Oprah will pay you *daily* until you find another zombie human?"

"Yeah. She wants to interview one on her show."

"Sam! We're rich—again. With your two thousand a day, plus expenses—don't forget to bill her for those—and the pittance the *Midley Beacon* makes, we'll have more money than ever before!"

"That sounds good."

"What's the matter? Did your dog die or something?"

"It's just that I've got the feeling that Oprah wants a zombie for something other than an interview. I feel uneasy at not knowing."

"Aha! An ulterior motive. Sam, you can count on it. People always have a hidden agenda. See if you can find out what it is, and we will publish an exposé on the *Midley Beacon*. You'll get paid for that too."

"OK. So it's like a double assignment: find Oprah her zombie and find out why she wants one, besides an interview."

"Right!"

* * *

Sam hit speed dial for Beefy Farm the next morning. "Hi, Bryan! This is Sam Melvin."

"Hi, Sam! Nice to hear from you. What's up?"

"Well, are you still non-zombie?"

"Sure. Was there a chance I'd revert?"

"Not that I know of. But I'm a little disappointed. If you were still a zombie, I could get you interviewed by Oprah Winfrey."

"That'd be cool. To tell you the truth, I miss it. I'm not as strong or energetic. But Doris is happier, so I'm good."

"You wouldn't happen to know any other zombies floating around Keokuk, would you?"

"Not a one. But then, no one knew about me. Thanks for hiding my identity in your article, by the way."

"Maybe I'll put out a classified ad for a zombie."

"You can put it in the *Keokuk Register*. They've called me just this morning to ask if I was the zombie in the *Midley Beacon*. They called all the beef farmers in the area."

"You didn't tell them? They contacted the *Midley Beacon* too."

"Nah. I just said, 'You've got to be kidding. Why would there be a zombie in Keokuk?'"

"So I'll advertise there. It's worth a try. I can also put it on Craigslist. 'Are you a zombie with red eyes? Contact Sam Melvin for fame and fortune.' Thanks, Bryan. See you when I see you."

"Bye."

Sam submitted his ad to Craigslist and the *Keokuk Register*. Then he sorted through the 349 emails in his detective inbox. He grouped them into *spam, clients, useless,* and *interesting.*

Ninety percent spam, as usual. Three potential clients. Could he work for two clients at once? *I'd better not. I can barely handle one client at a time.*

More emails had come in while he'd deleted his first batch. *Hmmm. Should I continue reading them or try something different?* He opted for different.

He called Dr. Galloway of the Turkey Institute. "Hi, Ed! This is Sam."

"Hi, Sam. I was just thinking of you as I read this morning's *Midley Beacon.* So that was your source for zombie blood, a farmer in Keokuk?"

"Yup. That's why I called you. I sent that sample to Dr. Marchanne Herbst in the Mayo Clinic."

"Yes. She's a geneticist specializing in human blood."

"Could you give me her number?"

"Sure."

Sam immediately called Dr. Herbst.

"Hi, Dr. Herbst, this is Sam Melvin. I sent you the sample of human zombie blood."

"Oh, thanks, so much. I'm sure that'll be an interesting field of study."

"Could you answer some questions about it?"

"I'm sorry, but my schedule is busy for the next six weeks. That's the soonest I'll be able to study it."

"Do you think the blood might cause other people to get the zombie disease?"

"Probably. It's a bacterial infection. But I can't say for sure until we test it."

"Could I test it? I have a volunteer who wants to try it."

"That would be completely outside any scientific protocol. I couldn't live with that."

"Could you just return part of the sample? We sent you twenty cc's."

"Perhaps. Let's see how many tests I'll need." She started counting. "I'll need at least fifteen cc's. I'd like the rest in case I think of more tests to run."

"Can't you even spare one cc?"

"Since you gave it to me originally, I don't think I can say no. What's your address? The same Keokuk address on the return label?"

"Yes, use that."

"All right. I'll send you one cc, frozen, to that address, today."

"Thanks, Dr. Herbst."

"You're welcome."

Sam sighed. If worse came to worse, he could try to reinfect Bryan and send him to Oprah. Or maybe there was a zombie in his inbox.

Four promising emails claimed to be zombies. Sam video called the first, meg489@frontier.com—Meg Quillion. *That sounds like a pen name.*

"Hello?" The video remained blacked out. Sam showed his. Some people knew his face.

"Hi, Meg. This is Sam Melvin, zombie detective. I put out an ad for human zombies, and I got an email from you saying you thought you might be one."

"Oh, hi, Sam! I never thought I'd actually hear from you. Well, every morning I wake up feeling dead. I stagger out of bed, and I can't think until I have a cup of coffee."

"Are these recent symptoms?"

"Yes, over the last couple of years, since I turned forty."

"Could I see your face?"

"I don't have any makeup on."

"All I want is to see your eyes."

"OK." The video camera came on, showing one brownish-hazel eye. It was bloodshot but not zombie red.

"That's enough. You're definitely not a zombie, Meg. I've seen an actual human zombie before."

"At least I got to talk to the famous Sam Melvin. Say hi to Lisa for me. Tell her I love her editorials."

"Will do. Bye."

The next guy was Zombie2000@aol.net. No other name, just a short "I'm sure I'm a zombie." When the video came up, a balding, heavyset man in a leather jacket, full beard, and abundant tattoos answered. He wore dark sunglasses.

"Hi, Sam Melvin here. Are you Zombie2000?"

"Yeah, that's me."

"You said you're sure you're a zombie."

"Yeah. See my tattoo?" He opened his leather jacket and showed a zombie tattoo on his hairy chest.

"That wasn't quite—"

"And my colors." He turned around and showed the same zombie image on the back of his jacket.

"I wasn't looking for biker clubs. I wanted a genuine human zombie."

"That's stupid. They're just make-believe, like Hollywood."

"You know the zombie turkeys were real last year."

"Yeah, but that was just a disease."

"Right. So is human zombiism. I met one last week."

"Did he eat your brains?"

"Uh, no." Sam felt his head to make sure it was intact. "We cured him, and now I have a client who wants to meet one."

"I'll ask the members of my club if they see one and call you if we do."

"Thanks, Mr., uh, Zombie. Look for red eyes."

"Like these?" He took off his sunglasses, and they were bruised and bloodshot, far worse than Meg's eyes.

"No. I want glowing red eyes. What happened to you?"

"Oh, I got into a fight after the bars closed last night. I have red eyes most mornings."

"I hope you get better."

"Ha! I'm already better than the other guy."

"I suppose that's something. Thanks for your time, Mr. Zombie."

"Just call me Big Z. That's what the gang does."

"Nice to meet you, Big Z. Bye."

The other two zombie candidates were a drug addict and an insurance salesperson.

That ad was a failure—so far. Let's try to find out why Oprah wants a zombie.

"Hi, Oprah. This is Sam."

"Hi, Sam. What's the good word?"

"No zombies yet, but I'm following up on my leads. This may take weeks."

"That's fine. This interview will be worth it. I'll televise it on my show *Oprah: Where Are They Now?*"

"On your OWN network?"

"You bet."

"OK, Oprah, I'll keep working on it."

"Thanks, Sam. There's no one else who can do what you do."

"Thanks. You really are uplifting, just like on TV."

After he put down his phone, Lisa looked at him. "What's the matter?"

"How do I investigate the world's most famous female billionaire?"

"Just like anyone else. Stake out her house."

"Which one? She's got nine."

"Wherever she is now."

"She's currently at her main home in Montecito, California. She might go to Maui or any of her other homes."

"We haven't done a stakeout together in a long time. The weather in Midley is crappy. Let's go stake out her home in Montecito and follow her wherever she goes."

"OK, Lisa. I'll plan a stake out, but I don't like it."

"You don't have to like it. Just do it. I'll arrange the plane tickets for tomorrow."

* * *

"Sam, we're leaving on the red-eye out of Bloomington tonight at nine p.m." Lisa looked up from her omelet the next morning, holding some cheesy eggs on her fork.

"Thanks. I'll pull things together."

"Let me see your packing list. I don't want to forget the night vision goggles. "

"Right. That's how we staked out Corn-All's dump." Sam hesitated. "Do you really think this is necessary?"

"What? Do you mean the stakeout? Of course! Trust me."

"Why don't we just ask her?"

"You expect to get at ulterior motives that way? You called her and didn't even ask."

"I know . . . She trusts me. I feel bad about stalking her."

"You're not stalking—you're investigating. You've got a license for that."

"But my own client? And we don't know what security she has in place."

"You're right about the security. We've got to assume the worst—the world's tightest security. See if you can get to see her. We'll go together. Then when we leave, we can hide out inside her estate."

"I don't know about this."

"It'll be great. Just like a spy movie or an old episode of *Mission Impossible*."

There was no persuading Lisa. Maybe he'd think of something else. Something ethical.

* * *

"Hi, Oprah. I got another eleven potential zombies I interviewed today. None of them were real zombies. I'm also pursuing getting some zombie blood."

"That sounds interesting. What are you going to do with it?"

"I talked with Dr. Marchanne Hebst of the Mayo Clinic, and she said it may cause another human to become a zombie. Then you'd have your zombie interview."

"I guess that'd work, but who'd take it?"

"The guy who was already a zombie. He misses the energy he had."

"Sam, you're worth every penny I pay you. Keep it up! You're giving me hope."

"I've got a surprise for you too. Lisa and I are coming to your mansion in Montecito tomorrow."

"That is a surprise. Why is that?"

"Lisa thinks we'll be able to better research human zombies after we talk to you in person."

Oprah peered at her tablet. "Hmm. I can make room for you on my schedule at three thirty p.m. tomorrow, California time."

"We'll be there! Bye."

Oprah was clearly uncomfortable with their self-invitation to her home. He chickened out from asking her anything further. Let Lisa do that. She was good at asking rude questions.

* * *

They arrived in Santa Barbara the next day and drove over to Oprah's mansion. At 3:30 sharp, the electric gate opened for them, and they drove into her spacious garage, lined with luxury cars. Oprah met them with a big smile.

"Thanks for coming all this way. Just park there next to the Bentley. Don't hit it. It's a gift."

"No problem, Oprah. I drove through turkey guts. I think I can handle a garage."

"I hope you didn't bring any zombie turkeys along?"

"Nope. We left them in Illinois. If you ever want any, let me know. There are hundreds caught every day." Sam and Lisa got out of the rental car. He left his fedora on the seat.

"So let's go into my kitchen dining area. It's where I feel most at home. I hope you will too."

Oprah led them to an open kitchen. They smelled fresh coffee and baking cookies.

"It does smell like home," Lisa said.

"It is. I had my chef make these for you. I've got to watch my weight."

"I never watch my weight, except when I look down at my belt." Sam patted his stomach as he picked up a cookie from the dish on the granite countertop.

"And I spend so much time chasing after Sam, I don't have a weight problem."

"I wish I had your slim figure, Lisa. I've had a lifelong struggle with my weight."

"I've always been a high-energy person, more focused on my goals than on eating."

"Me too, but I've always found time for eating. And comfort."

"I'm with Sam on that. Eating's just fuel for me. I don't get emotional comfort from it."

"That's unusual. Where do you get your emotional support?"

"Mostly I don't need it. But all the support I need comes from Sam."

"It sounds like a marriage made in heaven!"

"More like in the zombie turkey apocalypse," Sam put in.

"Lately, I've realized I've depended upon Sam since high school. He's been my most reliable reporter. And then during the turkey apocalypse, when he risked death for me, I knew I had to make our relationship permanent."

"This is just like our interview on the show! But speaking of zombies, what do you need to know that you had to see me in person?"

"We were wondering if there was more to your desire to interview this zombie person than just the interview?" Lisa said.

"Like what?"

"Do you have any other projects planned for this person, other than just the interview?"

"The interview would be big enough. You realize there's only been one documented case of zombiism in people, and you and Sam found it. There's never been an interview with a zombie before. That would send the ratings of my network and YouTube channel skyrocketing."

"I can understand that. Sam and I have seen our YouTube channel go viral over zombie stories."

Sam swallowed the last bite of his cookie, took a swallow of excellent black coffee, and said, "Um, Oprah, there was a zombie interview before."

"Oh? Where?"

"On the *Midley Beacon*, where I interviewed that cattle farmer."

"Yes, from Keokuk. I tried to find him."

"I promised I would protect his privacy."

"Of course."

"But when I asked you about the interview, Oprah, you sounded like the idea hadn't occurred to you. What were you thinking of originally when you called me?"

"Ah. That." Oprah sighed. "Mostly it was my own curiosity. When I read about his increased energy and appetite—well, I'll let you in on a secret."

"What?"

"I'm no spring chicken anymore. I'm sixty-two, and I don't have as much energy as I used to. It's harder to keep the weight off than ever, and I feel like exercising less than ever."

"Isn't all that just normal?" Sam asked.

"Yes, but I've fought against what is normal and expected all my life. I'm not going to stop now."

"But how is interviewing a zombie going to help?"

"If I can find out how he became a zombie, maybe I can too. At least long enough to lose some weight."

"Perhaps I'll be able to help you. I've already ordered a dose of zombie blood back from the Mayo Clinic. My former zombie agreed to take it again. We'll see if that works."

"Oh wonderful, Sam! But there's still a mystery here—how did this man originally get the zombie disease?"

"Sam, that'll be your next assignment—find out how he got it."

"But, Lisa, we already know. He got it from his breakfast grits. That's made by Corn-All."

"What!? I didn't know that." Oprah dropped her chocolate chip cookie.

"I put it in my story."

"I guess that's my fault," Lisa said. "I cut it from your story. We needed the space for an advertisement. Also, I try to keep all the stories under five hundred words. That's all people have the patience to read these days. Anyway, it didn't seem important, and it was speculative. We don't *know* that caused the zombiism."

"I can see we've got more work to do."

"Yes, you do, Sam. Oprah, thanks for giving us your time and your thinking beyond this interview. This'll give us more stories to cover."

"I was going to invite you to stay the night in my guest house. Are you just going to fly back tonight?"

"Yes. Duty calls. I can smell the coffee of the *Midley Beacon* newsroom pulling me back to work. And of course, Sam has his critical assignment for you."

"Don't you ever take breaks?"

"That'd be normal. Didn't you just say you spent your whole life fighting against normal?"

"I was speaking of social injustices, like gender and racial inequity."

"I fight against human limitations, especially my own. And now Sam's."

"Hey, Lisa, I'm still human. Remember that."

"I do, Sam. That's why I love you. You're a normal person for me to ground myself."

Oprah dabbed her eye. "I'm tearing up. I wish I had a camera going."

"You can always use your security cameras," Lisa said.

"Oh. How do you know about them?"

"I just assumed your whole property is thick with them. It's why we invited ourselves to your home. I couldn't see how we could spy on you to find out your secret reasons for the interview."

"That's certainly . . . honest. I'm glad you just asked me. I can see how I need to be honest in this investigation with my zombie detective. All right, I'll let you go this time, but you've got to promise to come back."

"We'd love to, Oprah. Just for your cookies and coffee, if not for you." Sam finished his coffee.

"That sounds good to me too. I'd be fun to feature you in the *Midley Beacon*."

"I'd be honored. I'll have my publicist contact you with the necessary contracts for an interview."

"We're always open. You've got our emails, mine and Sam's." Lisa handed Oprah her card and Sam offered her his.

"Let's go, Sam. I think we can catch the six p.m. flight to Chicago."

* * *

Sam called Bryan the next morning.

"Hi, Sam! I was just going to call you."

"Oh? Did you get the blood sample?"

"Yep. And I've already injected it, and I'm a zombie again!"

"That's great! You sure moved fast. Are you ready to be interviewed by Oprah?"

"Sure. My neighbor will take care of our cows. We help each other out when we go on vacation. I assume Doris can come too?"

"Sure. Oprah's got the money. Lisa and I will fly too. Let me give Oprah the good news. I'll have to tell Dr. Herbst too. She'll be interested in the results."

"Great. Let me know the date she wants me on the show. I'll drive to St. Louis to fly there."

"Will do. Bye."

Dr. Herbst or Oprah first? It's six a.m. California time. Dr. Herbst. Sam called her.

"Hi, Sam. Did you get the sample all right?"

"Yes. I've got good news for you—it worked."

"What does that mean?"

"The original zombie human turned zombie again."

"Oh my. I knew that's what you wanted, but I didn't really expect it to work after the blood had been frozen and thawed again."

"I guess these zombie bacteria are tough."

"I'll have to move up my research schedule on your blood sample. I can't wait to find out more about this bacterium." Dr. Herbst's voice rose with excitement.

"I'm glad to hear that. I just wanted to let you know Dr. Herbst. Bye."

Sam hummed happily as he deleted his spam email. Then he read the one from the Zombie Turkey Growers Association. Oh no.

Chapter 8 – ZTGA

"Lisa! Lisa!"

"Sam, calm down. You're going to hyperventilate."

"I'm already hyperventilating. We've got a problem."

"No problem is so great it can't be improved with some coffee." Lisa took a gulp. "Now, what is it?"

"The Zombie Turkey Growers Association."

"The ZTGA? That's the organization started by Hank Williams and his wife, Betty. What's their problem?"

"They're being sued as an unsafe work environment."

"Those farms can't be any more dangerous than a steel mill. Don't they have safety fencing?"

"Yes, but they don't have the funds to fight off the lawsuits. They're being sued in every state they operate. Also, those state legislatures are proposing laws to ban zombie turkey breeding."

"That's definitely a story for the *Midley Beacon* to cover, but why are you yelling? I haven't seen you this worked up since the turkeys were chasing you up the stairs at the Shakespearean Theatre at Navy Pier."

"They want to hire me as their expert witness to testify on their behalf."

"Great. You've got another gig."

"But I don't know anything about these legal shenanigans." Sam spread his hands in exasperation.

"You don't have to. Just testify about turkeys. You're the classic expert witness."

"But if they lose, our friends Hank and Betty will be out of business. It'll be on my shoulders."

"Nah. It's probably more the quality of their lawyers. Hmm, if they're seriously outspent, they'll lose. This is a problem."

"How can we fight them?"

"Who's their opposition?"

"A group called Concerned Citizens of Illinois."

"That's probably a front organization to hide who's really behind these suits. I've got an idea." Lisa rubbed her chin.

"What?"

"How you can win a lawsuit when you're outspent?"

"How?"

"Enlist the power of the press. Influence public opinion. Show everyone these guys are crooks. OK, Sam, I'm hiring you as a zombie detective to find the source of their money. I'm sure they're corrupt. It's the oldest rule in journalism—follow the money."

"OK. But I've never had two clients at once before."

"Great. It'll be a growth experience for you too."

"Thanks. I should give you a family discount."

"Don't bother. The *Midley Beacon* is making more money, so I need to spend more money to reduce my income taxes. This will be perfect."

"That's legal?"

"As legal as running a zombie turkey farm. Or avoiding paying income tax."

"There may be another problem."

"What?"

"ZTGA itself is a front group. Hank and Betty are the national leaders, but there are dozens of survivalist zombie turkey farmers who want to keep out of the public eye."

"Hey, you're a detective or private eye. Keep it private."

* * *

Sam walked home, barely noticing the occasional car on Midley's Main Street. *How do I start? Who's behind Concerned Citizens of Illinois? I suppose I'll search the internet.*

Sam found that the CCOI had been created late the previous year after the zombie turkey sausage online sales had taken off. *Hmmm. That's interesting.* No person was listed. He'd see what Wikipedia said. Oh, here was the CCOI home page.

Sam read their manifesto against zombie turkey farms. Most of it was based on the zombie turkey apocalypse that struck the US the previous year. It tied the dangers of zombie turkeys to the farms, but without any current evidence.

Sam studied their map of the threatening farms. Each farm had a five-mile-radius circle, showing the area of danger. He found Hank and Betty's farm in Henry. Examining all the farms across Illinois, Sam doubted they had them all.

I'm getting distracted. Who's behind them? No contact names, just an email. And a Facebook link. I'm there every day. Now I get paid for it.

Sam went to their page and found dozens of people ranting against zombie turkeys. He joined the group and posted an innocent question.

"I'm researching the history of CCOI. Can anyone tell me how it was founded?" There. He should learn something that way.

Sam found dozens of affiliated organizations all across the US. Whew! He had his work cut out for him. He asked each of them how they started.

Sam documented the founders of each of the twenty-seven organizations in twenty-one states. He gave each a call and an email. Why did you start? How did you start? How did you collect money? Can I join?

A pattern emerged. All started abruptly right around the success of Tom Tuffield's Online Zombie Turkey Sausage. All were cagey about their funding, protecting people's privacy.

Sam decided to create his own anti–zombie turkey organization. His would be different—not ruining people's livelihoods, but uncovering corruption. How could he attract donors? He was the zombie turkey expert of experts! He had instant credibility.

Several organizations offered to help, including help filing the founding legal documents as a nonprofit agency. He set up the public founding charters and legal documentation for the Zombie Turkey Apocalypse Prevention Society, ZTAPS for short. Then he sent out funding requests, prominently mentioning he was *the* Sam Melvin, zombie turkey reporter.

The money poured in. Sam documented each source, guaranteeing their anonymity. He planned to fold the nonprofit and never spend any of the money—he'd return it all. Sam traced the sources without result. His biggest donations came from other anti–zombie turkey organizations. He reached out to them again, trying to find a person behind each emolument. They all stonewalled him.

Finally he got a phone call from CCOI leader, Maci Armbruster. She'd been very supportive and was probably his best contact within the anti–zombie turkey community.

"Hi, Sam."

"Hi, Maci, what's up?"

"I really appreciate all the work you've put into ZTAPS. I know you want to find more donors. They're so essential when you're just starting out. I can't officially tell you my sources, but I can give you a tip: try raising money through the American Turkey Federation."

"Ah. I haven't tried them yet. I'll give it a shot."

Sam touched bases with his local ATF organization and asked for an interview. He drove to Bloomington and met with the local president, Sean Dahlquist. Sam explained ZTAPS and his desire to raise money through ATF members.

"I think some of our members may want to contribute. I'll bring it up at our meeting tomorrow," Sean said.

Sean did, and Sam saw a surge of donations. Then he got a visit from a national ATF official at lunchtime at their home in Midley. Lisa always worked through lunch.

Sam answered the door, and a man in a trench coat, dark glasses, and a hoodie stood there.

"Sam Melvin?"

"Yes?"

"I'm with the ATF. Could I come in? I'd like to discuss a donation."

"Sure. Come into my office, Mr. . . ."

"Smith. Call me Mr. Smith."

"OK, Mr. Smith." Sam could barely keep the scare quotes from his tone. This smelled fishy.

Mr. "Smith" kept his hoodie and glasses on in the house. "We've taken notice that you founded ZTAPS, and we'd like to help. We have a standard format that works well in our nationwide campaign against zombie turkeys." He opened his leather briefcase and handed Sam a binder.

"Here's the charter and board of governance we recommend. Take a look. Take as long as you'd like." He leaned back like he expected to wait.

Sam read the governance documents. "I'd be the president of the organization? But I'm the only member so far."

"Read on."

"So I'd get twelve ATF members immediately, who'd recruit more members? That's great." Sam skimmed the material. "An advertising budget? A web budget? And salaries? You'll pay me a hundred grand per year to be president?"

"Yes. Of course, that includes the annual two-week Anti-Zombie Forum in Hawaii this year. All expenses paid, for two. You are married to Lisa Kambacher, right?"

"Yes, but she took Melvin when we married."

"Kambacher is still her business name on the Midley incorporation papers. She hasn't legally changed it."

"Oh." *I'll have to verify this with Lisa.* Sam kept reading.

"Organization policy changes must be ratified by the board majority. What policies? Here they are. Policy number one: eradication of all zombie turkey farms. Well, that's pretty clear."

"Naturally we can't make that public. Neither can you. As ZTAPS' president, you're obligated to support all the policies."

Sam read them all. "Policy 26: all policies are kept strictly within ZTAPS.' That's the last one. Well. You've certainly given me a ton to think about. I'll want to consult with my wife, of course."

"That's fine. She's just down the street. Give her a call."

"She's working. Can't you come back tomorrow?"

"No. This is not negotiable. This is our one offer of support. If you don't sign this before I leave, I take the proposal with me and we blacklist your organization forever."

"OK. I hear you loud and clear. Let me call Lisa." Sam speed-dialed.

"Hi, Lisa."

"Spit it out. I don't have time."

"I have an offer of major funding for ZTAPS from the American Turkey Federation."

"How 'major'?"

"One hundred thousand a year salary for me, plus perks and benefits for both of us."

"Sam! You've done it! You've found the source of the anti-zombie money!"

"So should I not sign it?"

"Of course you should sign it."

"I don't understand."

"I'll be right there."

"Bye." Sam spoke into the silence. Lisa had already hung up.

"Well? What's the verdict?"

"Lisa's coming right over. She's my financial guru. I'm only a gumshoe."

"How long is this going to take? I'm parked outside. Will I get a ticket?"

"There's free parking all along Main Street." Sam glanced at his watch. "Twelve thirty. Louie'll be at Simon's Bar and Grill drinking a cold one with a hamburger. Louie's our local sheriff."

The door banged open. "Sam! My darling!" Lisa ran to Sam and smacked him on the lips. Then she looked up. "Oh? Who is this?"

"Mr. Smith of the ATF."

"Hi, Mr. 'Smith.'" Lisa didn't hide her scare quotes. She clearly didn't believe him.

"Ms. Kambacher." He shook her hand.

"That's Mrs. Melvin to you."

"Your legal name is still Kambacher."

"Yeah, so what? It's too much trouble to change legally."

"Sam tells me you're his financial advisor. Please examine this document and tell him to sign it. It's only good while I'm here. And I'll leave in thirty minutes."

"A time limit, eh? Good thing I'm a speed reader." Lisa scanned the pages. Her scowl grew as she read. She scanned down the policy page and flipped it back to Mr. Smith.

"As it is, you'll have to pay both Sam and me a hundred thousand. We're in this together. You'll get the *Midley Beacon* as a powerful internet platform for your policies."

"Perhaps something can be worked out. I can draw up a separate contract for each of you."

"No. We're one legal entity."

"I'll have to call my superiors to make this change." He stepped out the front door.

"Privacy must be very important to him. It's near zero out there. You ready to sign, Sam?"

"No way! I'd be bound to follow their policies contractually. No way am I going to betray the ZTGA as clients."

"Don't worry. You won't be bound by this piece-of-crap contract. Just trust me, and we'll nail these guys' hides to the wall."

"Lisa! I can't!"

"Just trust me," she whispered as Mr. Smith reentered.

His dark glasses fogged up, but he didn't take them off. He felt his way back to his seat across Sam's desk.

"Good news, Sam, Lisa. My boss has approved the contract modification. He'll pay each of you a hundred thousand, plus four weeks of seminars annually at Hawaii, London, and Paris.

Plus all your organization's expenses. That includes the *Midley Beacon's* costs."

"Now you're talking! Sam, let's sign."

"I don't understand."

"Just sign your legal name, 'Samuel Q. Melvin.'"

"What's the 'Q' for?" Mr. Smith's brows furrowed, shifting his dark glasses.

"Quincy. It's a family name. They came from Quincy, Illinois, and founded a farm here in Midley."

Sam felt nauseated. He thought he knew what Lisa was doing, but it seemed dodgy. He decided to trust her. She hadn't actually done anything illegal—yet.

"There. Samuel Q. Melvin, on the dotted line."

"Now put down, Lisa Kambacher," Mr. Smith said.

"Of course." Lisa signed with a flourish.

Mr. Smith broke into a big smile and grabbed the contract. "I'll make a copy of this for you two. I can take off these now." He removed his dark glasses and hoodie, showing a handsome, dark-haired man with big brown eyes. "And my real name is Leveret Poynter. Just call me Lev. We're in the ATF together now." He shook their hands. "Let me notarize this." He got out his stamp and signed his name on the contract.

"Sorry to run off, but duty calls. I've got to get this to our legal and personnel office. Expect your first paychecks on the first of next month. To tide you over, here's a small advance." He handed her a check.

"Ten thousand dollars?" Sam asked.

"Do we have to report this to the IRS? This isn't a paycheck." Lisa looked into Lev's eyes.

"Do as you please. The ATF is recording this as 'negotiating expense' on my expense report."

"Ah. I get it."

"Bye!" Lev waved cheerily and went out the door.

"OK, Lisa, come clean. I get the fact my signature isn't legally binding, since my legal name is 'Sam Melvin,' not 'Samuel Q. Melvin.' What about 'Lisa Kambacher'? I thought you legally changed it when we married."

"I did, but I didn't change any of my incorporations. I use Lisa Kambacher as a legal alias."

"Aren't you still legally bound then?"

"Not really. I signed 'Kambechar,' not 'Kambacher.' The turkey never noticed."

"This whole thing seems really shady. What about the ten thousand? We can't spend that."

"Why not? It's a bribe or gift, obviously. I doubt it's even recorded on their books. This is a private check from Leveret Poynter, not the ATF. No contractual obligation."

"So we're just going to double-cross them and break the contract?"

"We have no contract as Sam and Lisa Melvin nor as my alias Lisa Kambacher, our legal names. We're going to expose their corruption. I'll edit the video from the security cameras and post it on YouTube tonight on our channel. And you'll collect your fees from ZTGA. And I'll cash the check and put it in my mad money account."

"What security cameras? When did we get security cameras?"

"I copied Oprah's security for our house. Very handy."

"When did you learn about her security?"

"When we went to the bathroom together at her house. We had some girl talk."

"What's this 'mad money' account? What's that all about?"

"When someone makes me mad, I make money off them. I then save that money for my retirement."

"Cool. How much do you have so far?"

"Only about half a million. Close your mouth, Sam. You look like you're catching flies."

"OK. I guess my investigation for ZTGA is done. Thanks for the help, Lisa."

"That's what wives are for."

"I still have to testify as an expert witness at the civil trial."

"When's that?"

"Tomorrow, in Chicago."

"Do you have to do much to prepare?"

"Nah. I'll just testify about how safe their zombie turkey cages are. I know all about zombie turkeys."

"Watch out for cross-examination. Their lawyers will try to make you say something to incriminate the ZTGA. Don't say any more than you have to."

"That's always good advice."

"Why don't we knock off early and fly up to Chicago? We can have a mini-honeymoon. It'll be on me. I'll spend some of my mad money."

"You don't have to ask me twice!"

* * *

Sam and Lisa drove to the Chicago courthouse from their hotel and walked into the courtroom before the deposition started at 9:00 a.m. Sam did a double take as he saw Lev Poynter talking with a group of lawyers. Lev looked up and started as he saw Sam and Lisa. He excused himself and hurried over to them.

"Hi, Sam, Lisa. I didn't expect to see you here. Are you here to testify on behalf of Concerned Citizens of Illinois? Or your own ZTAPS?"

"Hi, Leveret. Sam will testify as an expert witness on zombie turkeys." Lisa smiled at him.

"Oh, that's great. You're certainly an expert. I look forward to it."

"We are too. We're about to start. We've got to get seated."

"Say, Lisa"—Sam nudged her arm—"there are Hank and Betty. Too bad I didn't get a chance to talk with them."

"You can talk afterward. Since they're the defendants, as the expert witness you can't show partiality."

"Oh, right. When does this trial begin? It's past nine."

"The lawyers are conferring with the judge right now. It's not a trial. You're giving evidence on zombie turkeys as part of the discovery process. The Concerned Citizens of Illinois claims that zombie turkeys are too dangerous to domesticate and is trying to get all the zombie turkey farmers to quit—or put up a million-dollar bond."

"Yeah, I know that part. Hank and Betty told me."

The judge, Harold Dredd, introduced the lawyers for each side and summarized the case. "This is a deposition hearing where the defense will present their discoveries of evidence. The plaintiffs may cross-examine any witnesses. The first witness for the defense, Mr. Sam Melvin."

After he was sworn in, the defense lawyer for ZTGA, Mr. Slate Slatley, spoke. "Mr. Melvin, please state your occupation."

"I'm a zombie detective."

"Any kind of zombies?"

"Yes. I've worked with squirrels, cows, turkeys, and humans."

"What was your former occupation?"

"I was the lead reporter for the *Midley Beacon*."

"What sorts of stories did you cover as a lead reporter?"

"Mostly zombie turkey stories. I didn't get promoted to lead reporter until after the zombie turkey apocalypse last year."

"And that occurred when?"

"Early November. By Thanksgiving it had spread all over the US."

"When you reported on zombie turkeys, how close did you get to them?"

"Too close."

The lawyers chuckled.

"I believe that. Exactly how close was that?"

"Let's see. Once a turkey poked its head through a crack in the car window. Another time one flew at me, and I grabbed it by its neck and wrung its head off. You can't get any closer than that, hand-to-beak battling."

"Now how about your current job as a zombie detective. How close have you gotten to zombie turkeys there?"

"There was my visit to the Tuffield turkey farm. I got closer to them than to you."

"Did you feel endangered?"

"Not really. They were all behind steel wire cages or fences."

"So all the danger you faced was from zombie turkeys in the wild, but not from domesticated zombie turkeys?"

"That's right."

"No more questions, Your Honor."

"Thank you, Mr. Slatley. Your witness, Mr. Grover."

Garrison Grover, the lawyer for CCOI, smiled. "You've certainly have had an exciting career."

"Well, since the zombie turkeys came along." Lisa spluttered in the audience. Sam had a sinking feeling he shouldn't have said anything.

"Indeed. What did you cover before the zombie turkeys came along?"

"Um, local news for Midley, Illinois."

"Like what? Give me an example."

"Mrs. Huntington's award-winning afghans. The Jonas Brothers concert in Peoria."

"So no danger there. Is that right?"

"Unless you got between Jonas Brothers' fans and the stage." This time the lawyers laughed aloud. Even Judge Dredd smiled.

"But not like zombie turkeys. Would you say they helped your career?"

"Objection! Leading the witness." Mr. Slatley looked from Mr. Grover to Judge Dredd.

"Objection sustained. Reword the question, Mr. Grover."

"Mr. Melvin, did your career improve after the zombie turkey apocalypse?"

"I got promoted."

"Why was that?"

"I broke all the major stories during the apocalypse."

Lisa smiled at him.

"Yes, you did. And your personal life—did you marry Ms. Kambacher after the apocalypse?"

"Yes." Sam felt nauseous. He didn't like where this was going.

"So on the whole, you were better off after the zombie turkey crisis than before?"

"Objection!" Mr. Slatley said.

"Your Honor, I'm trying to establish bias here."

"Objection overruled. The witness will answer the question."

"I guess from a personal point of view, I am definitely better off married to Lisa."

"And from a professional point of view, did you prefer reporting on zombie turkeys or Mrs. Huntington's afghans? Or the Jonas Brothers?"

"It was definitely more exciting than the afghans. But I'd rather go into a crowd of Jonas fans than zombie turkeys."

"From a detective point of view, are zombie turkeys a significant portion of your business?"

"What do you mean by 'significant'?"

"At least twenty percent."

"I guess so. They're about a quarter or so."

"So twenty-five percent of your income comes from zombie turkeys?"

"About."

"No more questions at this time, Your Honor."

Lev smiled and gave him a thumbs-up. The court reporter clicked away as Sam walked back to Lisa. He wasn't surprised to see her scowl. He sat down.

"You're too cooperative as a witness. Be hostile," she whispered in his ear.

"Sorry, Lisa."

"Let me show you how it's done."

"What?"

"Next witness, Ms. Lisa Kambacher."

"What?" Sam repeated.

Lisa walked to the witness stand, elegant in her stiletto heels and sheath skirt. After swearing in, Mr. Slatley approached.

"Ms. Kambacher, please state your occupation."

"Editor of the *Midley Beacon*."

"How long have you had that position?"

"Fifteen years."

"What sort of news does the *Midley Beacon* cover?"

"We're the premier source for all zombie news."

"What sorts of media does the *Midley Beacon* produce?"

"Paper newspapers, online news website, online Facebook page, online Instagram account, and YouTube channel."

"How often do you produce a YouTube video?"

"During breaking news, multiple times per day."

"I understand you published a YouTube video last night, at around midnight?"

"That's correct."

"And what was the subject of that video?"

"The lawsuit between ZTGA and CCOI." The CCOI lawyers took sharp breathes and leaned forward in their chairs.

"Your honor, I'd like to introduce this YouTube video as evidence. I will play it so the court reporter can record it."

"Go ahead, Mr. Slatley."

The video played on a flat-screen monitor. Lisa appeared in a navy suit and white blouse, with a red scarf at her neck.

"Breaking news tonight in the lawsuit between the Concerned Citizens of Illinois et. al. and the Zombie Turkey Growers Association. The *Midley Beacon* has discovered the CCOI and all of the associated plaintiffs across the country are secretly funded by the American Turkey Federation. The ATF is forming, funding, and manning organizations across the country to protest against zombie turkey growers. The motivation largely financial, since the skyrocketing growth of zombie turkey sausages and zombie turkey wings has eroded ATF members' market share."

The video showed a graph of AFT's declining market share and ZTGA's growing share.

Lisa appeared again. "The *Midley Beacon* has obtained this video of a negotiating session between the ATF agent and a newly founded anti-zombie group. The faces have been blurred to protect anonymity."

"And to prevent lawsuits and accusations of illegal taping," Lisa whispered into Sam's ear.

"This is an outrage! I demand that this video be stopped!" Mr. Grover shouted.

"Order in the court. This is being admitted as evidence. You may cross-examine Ms. Kambacher afterward. If there are any more outbursts, I'll have the bailiff escort you from the courtroom, Mr. Grover."

Fuming, Mr. Grover sat down. Lev Poynter's face rippled between embarrassment and poison as he looked at Sam and Lisa.

After the video finished, Judge Dredd asked, "Mr. Grover, do you have any questions for Ms. Kambacher?"

"Ms. Kambacher, how can you claim this has any bearing at all upon the ATF or the CCOI?"

"Check the court reporter's recorders. You'll find that both are mentioned in the video transcript."

"But there is no proof that an anonymous person is a representative of ATF. This could be a big charade enacted by your newspaper as a publicity stunt."

"Do you have a question?"

"Yes. What is your proof that this video is tied to the ATF or the CCOI?"

"I have more proof than this video. I have the signed document of the contract with the ATF and the signed check from the ATF's agent. They're in this envelope. Please admit these into evidence as well, Judge Dredd."

Slate Slatley took the envelope from Lisa and handed it to the judge.

"Wait! That isn't a valid contract," Grover said.

"There's Leveret Poynter's signature as an authorized member of ATF. And it's notarized." Lisa smiled smugly at him.

"But you are in breach of this contract."

"I don't believe so."

"Look at paragraph 13b—"

"Look at the signatures."

"Samuel Q. Melvin? Is that Sam Melvin?"

"No. I have a copy of Sam's birth certificate with me. May I admit that as evidence, Your Honor?" Lisa looked at Judge Dredd.

"Yes, Ms. Kambacher."

"Aren't you Lisa Kambacher? Isn't this your signature?" Grover gabbled.

"Yes and no. I am Lisa Kambacher, but that signature is Lisa Kambechar. It has no legal status at all. Here's my birth certificate, Judge."

Grover looked to the judge with dread. "I request a delay to determine a response to this new evidence."

"Any more evidence to present, Mr. Slatley?"

"No, your honor."

"Request granted. This deposition is adjourned."

Amid the hubbub of lawyers murmuring, Lisa said, "Sam, let's go talk with Hank and Betty."

"What did you give them? Their lawyer looked like he was going to faint." Betty hung on to Hank's arm as they met by the door.

"I gave them pure poison. We showed the ATF is funding all these protest groups across the country behind the scenes."

Slate Slatley joined them. "You certainly put a spoke in the wheels of their case, Lisa. But that may not be enough to derail them."

"Why not?"

"They can regroup and directly sue you as the ATF."

"Let them try. This video already has a million views on YouTube and is covered by CNN and the AP. The stink will sink them. I bet they'll drop the whole thing like a month-old fish. Oh, and this wasn't all me. I hired Sam as my zombie detective to smoke out the ATF. He got all the credit in the *Midley Beacon*."

"Thanks, Lisa." Sam beamed at her.

"I hope you're right, Lisa. The ATF is really ticked at you for tricking them with that contract. I think they'll do something."

"We'll just outsmart them again," Lisa said with certainty.

* * *

After celebrating in Chicago, Sam and Lisa drove back to Midley that night.

"I've got another assignment for you, from the *Midley Beacon*," Lisa said.

"What's that?"

"Find out how that GMO grain got into those grits. I'm hiring you to contact trace human zombiism."

"But I don't know how to do that!"

"You'll figure it out."

Chapter 9 – Contact Tracing

The next morning, before Lisa went to work, she said, "You don't mind me giving you work, do you, Sam?"

"Nah. It's just like I'm working for the *Midley Beacon*. Except I'm not paid."

"You're paid—just not by me, but by *Midley Beacon*. More accurately, by the pop-up ads on your articles. But keep writing those great stories for the *Beacon* about your cases, and I'll hire you back. It'll be cheaper than paying you piecework."

"Thanks, Lisa!"

At home, Sam settled behind his desk. How in the world would he discover how this happened? As his laptop powered up, he called Bryan Franklin.

"Hey, Bryan."

"Hi, Sam. Do you have the date yet for the Oprah interview?"

"Nope, not yet. How's being a zombie going?"

"Great. Even Doris has gotten used to it."

"I got another question."

"Shoot."

"You know that box of corn grits you had from Corn-All? Remember I said to save it?"

"Yeah. It's in my cupboard with a sticky note, 'Do Not Use.'"

"Could I take it? I want to try and see if I become a zombie by eating them."

"Wow, that's pretty wild, Sam. Why?"

"I want to force Corn-All to investigate its disposal methods. Obviously, their GMO corn got into their products after it was supposedly buried last Thanksgiving."

"I'm all for it. Do you want me to mail it to you?"

"Uh, sure. Send it by next-day delivery, and I'll reimburse you for the cost."

"No problem."

Sam reviewed his notes from his investigation of Corn-All's disposal last year with Lisa. He made a little chart of their process.

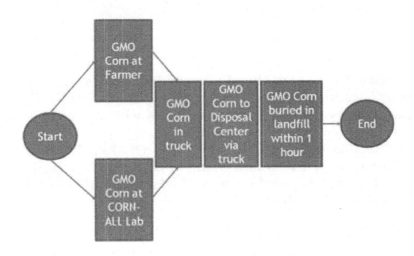

CORN-ALL DISPOSAL PROCESS

Sam studied his chart. He couldn't really see how the GMO corn got into the grits from this chart. He made another chart of how zombies came from the corn.

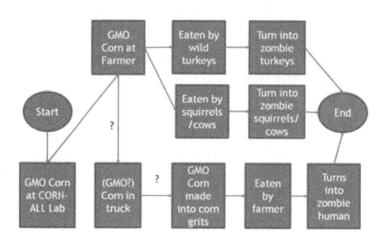

GMO CONTAMINATION PROCESS

Sam felt he had a handle on zombie turkeys, squirrels, and cows. But how did the GMO corn get into the grits? That was the mystery. Sam marked one arrow with a question mark. Now he knew where to start his investigation.

Sam looked in his contact list. Dr. Ken Wu. Research scientist for Corn-All and friend of Dr. Galloway. He'd helped with the corn disposal process. Maybe he could help with this.

"Hi, Dr. Wu. This is Sam Melvin."

"Hi, Sam. I see your name pop up in my news app from time to time. What's up?"

"I'm investigating Corn-All's Corn Grits. How do they get made?"

"They're produced at our factory in DeKalb, Illinois."

"How does the factory get the corn?"

"It comes from local farmers."

"How does it get there?"

"By truck. We have a rail spur, but that's mostly for shipping out of the state. For in-state traffic, we use trucks. Is that all? I've got a meeting I've got to get ready for."

"You've been a great help. Thanks. Bye."

I hope I'm right. I don't see how this helps much. Sam added to his contamination chart.

GMO CONTAMINATION PROCESS

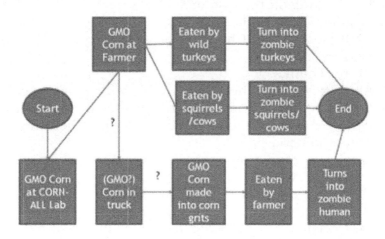

After studying his chart, Sam added another question mark. Now he had two unknowns. Did the GMO corn for the grits come from the lab or the farm? Sam didn't have the farmer's phone number where the GMO corn was originally grown, but it wasn't far from Midley. He'd just drive over there this afternoon and chat with him.

Sam scarfed down a quick burger, coffee, and apple pie at the local Midley burger joint. Then he drove south of Bartonville.

He knew exactly where the farm was but had never gone there before. He'd gotten the address from Dr. Galloway of the Turkey Institute: a Mr. and Mrs. Hall, RR 15. Dr. Galloway had investigated the farm and found the GMO corn there when he was tracing the origin of the zombie turkeys.

Sam had crisscrossed the area many times but had never stopped there. Now he'd finally go to the origin of the zombie turkeys.

Pulling into the farmhouse drive, he parked and went to the door. A slender lady in her fifties answered it.

"Hi, I'm Sam Melvin, an investigator hired by the *Midley Beacon*. Are you Mrs. Hall?"

"Yes."

"I'm researching the zombie turkey outbreak that happened near here. Do you mind if I ask you a few questions?"

"No, not at all. C'mon in out of the cold. Steve's in the garage, working on the tractor."

"Thanks, Mrs. Hall."

"Call me Beverly. I have a fresh pot of coffee. Would you like some?"

"Sure. Thanks."

After they sat at the kitchen table with mugs of coffee in front of them, Beverly asked, "What would you like to know? I thought we'd covered all the details last year when the Turkey Institute was here."

"Yes, I've read their report. I'm following up on what happened afterward."

"What do you mean?"

"What happened to the GMO corn you had?"

"The original test field was harvested and sent to Corn-All in October."

"How did it get shipped?"

"They wanted it kept separate from all the other corn, so we had it in a special crib. A Corn-All truck came and took it away."

"So the truck had Corn-All on the side?"

"Yes."

"Dr. Galloway said you still had some of the grain left over. What happened to that?"

"We had a partial bag left over after the harvest. Steve kept it next to the crib, but they didn't take it. When the scientists from the Turkey Institute came here, they asked if they could take it, and we said sure."

"That's just the info I needed." Sam looked at his chart on his tablet. He'd have to add a box showing GMO corn shipped to the Turkey Institute. He'd forgotten about that. Also, he'd have to find where this GMO corn went. What if some got into the production plant?

"Do you think Steve'll mind if I ask him a few questions?"

"No, he's friendlier than I am."

Beverly came with him out to the garage.

"Hi, honey! We got company. This is Sam Melvin, an investigator for the *Midley Beacon*.

"Hi, Sam. Sorry I can't shake your hand." He gestured with his oil-covered hands and went to a sink, where he washed up to his elbows.

"This is a good arrangement, having a heated garage. I could use it for my old Ford."

"Yup. We put in heat about twenty years ago. I'd gotten tired of working on my equipment in the cold." He shook Sam's hand vigorously. "Now what can I do for you?"

"Just checking up about that GMO corn that caused the zombie turkey plague. Your wife said the Corn-All truck picked it up."

"Yup. I was there when they did, last October eighteenth, I think. Do you need the exact date?"

"Sure."

"It's here on my phone. Nope, it was the nineteenth, a Monday."

"OK." Sam jotted that down. "So that truck was owned and operated by Corn-All?"

"Yup. I chatted with the driver. He'd been there over twenty years."

"Thanks. What about when the scientists came from the Turkey Institute?"

"Oh, you mean Northwestern University Poultry Institute?"

"Yes. Most people call it the Turkey Institute."

"Yeah, but one of the scientists was pretty sensitive about it. Anyway, they came and asked if they could take a sample of the grain, and I gave them the whole bag. Who wants grain that might create a zombie?"

"It'd be like a sitting time bomb."

"You got it, Sam. That's how I felt."

"So the scientists just took the bag with them?"

"Yup. I put it in their van myself."

"There was no more of the grain?"

"Nope. I filled the bag myself from sweeping up after the harvest and loading the crib from the harvest truck. I didn't know if Corn-All would want the sweepings or not."

"They didn't, but it helped the Turkey Institute a lot," Sam said.

"I'm glad."

"Well, that takes care of my questions. Thanks for your time"—Sam looked at Beverly—"and your coffee."

"Have a cup to go, Sam."

"Sure will. Thanks."

Sam thought about his next step on his way back to Midley. He needed to make sure the truck went to the Corn-All lab and not the factory. He'd call Dr. Wu. He also would make sure the bag got to the Turkey Institute. He'd call Dr. Galloway about that.

Both doctors confirmed the delivery of the grain to the lab and the college building. Dr. Wu even sent an electronic receipt. He also sent an electronic copy of the disposal record to the Illinois Waste Company. Dr. Galloway said the grain sack was still in the Turkey Institute lab, used for further testing.

Sam updated his chart with his new information. He got rid of some boxes and added some.

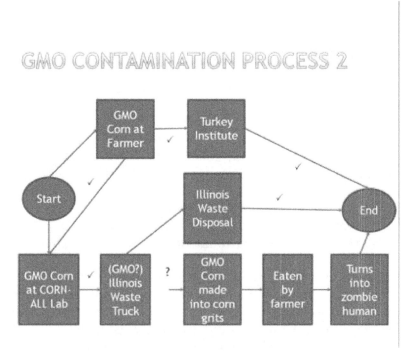

GMO CONTAMINATION PROCESS 2

Sam checked off the points that were clear now. The Turkey Institute wasn't the source, nor the farmer. The GMO grain was last seen leaving the Corn-All lab in an Illinois Waste truck.

He and Lisa had staked out their landfill overnight last November. No one picked up anything from there. They hadn't even seen raccoons at night. The mystery was whether the waste truck got to the landfill that day. He looked at the disposal record. November 11. The zombie turkey plague had just started. No one knew the GMO grain caused zombiism in turkeys—or humans.

He had no idea who ran the trucks that fed Corn-All their grain. He suspected they were independent operators. Time for a road trip to Corn-All and Illinois Waste.

Sam reviewed the video of their last visit. Their story had cleared Corn-All of all wrongdoing last year after investigating their disposal of the GMO corn. Nothing was taken out of the dump overnight. Even animals couldn't get the GMO corn, for it was covered within ten minutes by the next load.

Sam looked up Illinois Waste Management's phone number. Mindy Hawthorne. He remembered her. She was a twentysomething, eager to promote IWM.

"Hello, this is Illinois Waste Management."

"Hi. This is Sam Melvin. Could I speak with Mindy Hawthorne?"

"I'll transfer you."

"Hi, Sam! Thanks for your wonderful article about our services! I'm still using it in our promotional material."

"Hi, Mindy. I'm glad to talk to you again. Could I come by for another visit today? I'm investigating Corn-All corn, and I've got more questions."

"Sure thing, Sam, but we just deal with waste disposal here. We only get one or two loads from Corn-All a week."

"That's fine. I just want to talk with your truckers again. Say, do you do all your trucking yourself, or do you hire independent truckers?"

"Our trucks make regular runs to our customers. However, any customer may use their trucks to dispose of their waste."

"Does Corn-All use their trucks for their waste?"

"No, they're on our regular disposal run."

"OK, thanks. I'll be there after lunch."

"I'll be on the lookout for you."

* * *

Sam arrived at Illinois Waste in the early afternoon. He swallowed the last bite of an apple fritter he'd bought with his coffee to stay awake on his three-hour drive from Midley. Snacking with fresh, hot coffee on his expense account was one of the perks of his job with the *Midley Beacon*.

Mindy greeted him warmly at her office door. Her reddish-brown hair framed her smiling face. "Sam! I just reread your article before you came. You and Lisa did such a great job covering our operation. I really don't know what else to tell you."

"Oh, you don't have to tell me anything. Just let me nose around and ask questions."

"Great. Here's your visitor's card. You can go anywhere. Who do you want to question?"

"Probably the gate guards and the truckers again. We're investigating a different story than the zombie turkeys this time."

"OK. I'll be in some meetings, but call me if you need me for anything."

"Thanks, Mindy."

* * *

Sam walked up to the first trucker he saw bringing his load of dirt in the gate. The man lit a cigarette as he waited for his papers to be signed.

"Hi. Do you often drop your loads here?" Sam looked up at him in his cab.

"Yeah, this is the closest clean dump to our construction site."

"Do you ever run loads from Corn-All?"

"Yeah, they're over in DeKalb. Maybe a couple of times a year, when they have a construction project."

"How about the weekly loads they run?"

"No, that's all Illinois Waste drivers. I work for Mighty Construction."

"That's interesting. Can I get you a coffee?" Sam gestured to the coffee machine outside the guard's office.

"Sure. Thanks. Are you a trucker?"

Sam walked to the machine and bought a cup. "Nah. Well, I did drive the grain truck for my dad's farm through my teens." Sam handed him the cup.

"Next to the combine?"

"Yup, and then over to the grain silo. Dad never paid me, but he let me use his car and paid for the gas. I'm Sam, by the way."

"Hi, Sam. I'm Harley. I hope to start my own trucking company one day." The Illinois Waste guard stamped his papers.

"Well, good luck! Thanks, for chatting."

Harley drove into the yard and dumped. The next truck, an Illinois Waste one, pulled up to the gate.

"Hi. I'm Sam Melvin. Can I get you a coffee?" *Might as well try it again.*

"Hi, Sam. I'm Vince. Coffee's not for me. But I'd take a Caffeine Monster." The driver was a young man with shaggy blond hair and a beard.

"There's a pop machine. Let's see if they got it." Sam checked it out and called to the trucker, "How about Caffeine Explosion? That's all they got."

"Sure, I'd appreciate that."

"Here you go." Sam handed him the can through his window. "How d'ya like this Illinois Waste route?"

"Its Corn-All route is good, steady work. It's only tough in bad storms."

"Do you haul a lot of their grain?"

"Nah. Just waste from their office buildings."

"You've never gotten grain from their lab in DeKalb?"

"No. Some of the drivers have that job sewn up."

"What'dya mean?"

"We bid on the jobs by seniority. The senior guys like that route."

"Huh. I guess that makes sense, doing things by seniority." Sam looked at his tablet to check his old notes. "Would you know a Mark Victor?"

"Yeah. He's one of the senior drivers with that route. How'd you know him?"

"Oh, I met him last year during the zombie turkey apocalypse."

"That was really something. I drove through one of their flocks on I-55. Cracked my windshield."

"Yeah, that happened to my car too."

"Well, nice to meet you. I gotta go."

Sam sat down to think. Mark Victor had been the truck driver who'd hauled from Corn-All and dumped here last year. Could his load of grain have been highjacked? Stolen? How could Sam find out? He hadn't gotten Mark Victor's phone or address.

Sam focused on the Illinois Waste drivers, hoping to find Mark Victor. Most of them knew Mark, and they confirmed he had grain disposal.

Back at his hotel, Sam searched for Mark Victor on the internet and found nothing. In desperation, he searched on Facebook and found a Mark Victor, of Aurora, Illinois. Married, with two kids in high school. Worked at Illinois Waste. No address or phone.

Huh. I wonder if he's on LinkedIn? There he is. Twenty years at Illinois Waste and . . . what's this? Illinois Best Disposal Company. Five years there as Chief Logistics Officer? I wonder what that's all about?

Sam wrote up a report for Lisa, emailed it, and then called her.

"Hi, honey."

"Sam! I was just reading your email. Great work!"

"Thanks, Lisa. I'm a little stymied about how to investigate from here."

"Of course you should check for Illinois Best Disposal at Illinois Waste. Did they use them from the farmer in Bartonville?"

"Of course! I should have thought of that. I'll check with Mindy tomorrow."

"Is she hitting on you?"

"No, I think she's just friendly with everyone. That's her job as PR."

"She'd better not try anything. And you'd better not encourage her."

"*I only have eyes for you,*" Sam warbled.

"It's a good thing you're a better reporter than a singer, or you'd still be single."

"But you like my reporting and married me. That's what matters. Anyway, let's say we find Illinois Best Disposal did the disposal job from Bartonville. How do we approach Mark Victor?"

"Ooo! I've got a great idea. We'll hire Illinois Best Disposal to get rid of Midley's trash."

"How can you do that? I know you're on the city council and all, but I didn't know you did anything."

"There's not much work for a town of five hundred, but we still need waste disposal. Our contract is up this month, and the company is raising their prices. I'll put out a bid for Illinois Best."

"I saw the company website said, 'Lowest prices, guaranteed.'"

"Then it's a cinch, assuming they're telling the truth. Call me tomorrow as soon as you confirm they were in on the Corn-All disposal last year. Then I'll set the trap into motion.

"Will do!"

* * *

At the breakfast bar the next morning, Sam poured grits into his bowl and added hot water. He read "Good Grits" off the box Bryan had given him as he ate his first bite. *Stale. I wonder if I can doctor them up?* Sam added cream and maple syrup. *Not bad.* Along with bacon and sausages, he could get to like them this way. *I wonder if I'll turn zombie? I wonder how many it'll take?* He made a note in his journal: *One bowl Good Grits for breakfast.*

Back in his room, Sam called Dr. Wu at Corn-All.

"Hi, Dr. Wu. This is Sam Melvin."

"Hi, Sam. I only have a minute before I've got a meeting."

"No problem. I've just got one question. Are there any GMO grain disposals going on in the future, like you did with the GMO grain you got from Bartonville?" Sam deliberately avoided the word *zombie*, since Corn-All was very sensitive about that after the zombie turkey apocalypse.

"Um, yes. Later this week, from a Decatur farm."

"Could you send me that address? We want to track and prove the effectiveness of Corn-All's disposal methods."

"I guess so." He gave him the address.

"Thanks so much. Who tracks all these shipments at Corn-All?"

"That'd be our logistics department. Just call our main number and ask for them. I gotta go. Bye."

Sam called the logistics department next. He was routed to a public relations person, Ms. Harmony Goodbody. She had a very pleasant voice.

"How can I help you, Mr. Melvin?"

"Ms. Goodbody, I'm researching Corn-All's grain disposal methods for the *Midley Beacon*. I hope to prove their complete innocence in the incident of the GMO grain disposal last year, before the z—er, turkey outbreak. I wonder if I could look through your disposal schedules for November?"

"That's an unusual request. We must protect our client farmers' privacy. However, our contracts are a matter of public record. On the other hand, we must also protect our financial information. What exactly are you looking for?"

Sam could listen to her for hours. But he knew what he needed. "I don't need the farmers' names, just the pickup addresses and the dates. I also need the pickups from your research lab in DeKalb."

A moment of silence, and then, "I'll prepare a spreadsheet of the information. Do you want all of last November?"

"Yes, and October and December as well, if you don't mind."

"OK. I'll have to ask you to sign a nondisclosure agreement in person. You may not share these addresses with anyone."

"Except for your DeKalb facility."

"Oh. Yes. Of course."

"When can I sign the NDA and pick up this info?"

"I'll have it by lunchtime."

"Should I meet you by twelve at your Schaumberg headquarters?"

"That'll be fine."

"See you then, Ms. Goodbody."

He called Mindy Hawthorne. "Hi, Mindy. Mind if I come over this morning and talk to your drivers again?"

"Are you still researching your story on Illinois Waste Disposal?"

"You bet. It's going great."

"C'mon over. I love to see Illinois Waste in the news."

Sam drove to the Illinois Waste Disposal yard. By chatting with the truck drivers, he confirmed Dr. Wu's information that there was a disposal run this week from Decatur. None of the drivers had it, but they thought Mark Victor had the bid.

Good confirmation. And it only cost me six cups of coffee. Sam drove to Schaumberg headquarters of Corn-All.

Ms. Goodbody met him in the corporate lobby and handed him a folder with the printed spreadsheets. "I can't give you an electronic copy, but a printed copy is OK."

Sam stared at her. She was well named. Then he scanned through the sheets. There it was. Illinois Best Disposal picked up and dropped off a load of grain from the Corn-All lab on November 17.

"This is exactly what I need, Ms. Goodbody!"

"I'm glad I could bring you a little harmony."

Sam did a double take and then laughed. "I see what you did there! I've got to call this in. Thanks so much."

He called Lisa as he walked out of the lobby. "Hi, Lisa! I've confirmed that it was Illinois Best Disposal that took the grain from the lab to the Illinois Waste site."

"Great! I'll get on the horn and hire Illinois Best Disposal for Midley."

* * *

Back at the hotel, Sam had grits at the breakfast bar for lunch too. He figured the more he ate of it, the more likely he'd turn zombie.

Lisa called him. "Hi, Sam! We've got them. They'll drop down by Midley tomorrow afternoon."

"Hmm. That's the day they pick up grain for disposal from their Decatur lab."

"What time?"

"The previous pickup was a week ago, at eight a.m."

"Let's be there and track them and see what they do with it."

"OK, I'll check out now. I'll be there for supper."

* * *

Sam drove Lisa's Lexus to Decatur early the next morning after his third straight breakfast of corn grits. Lisa had declined his breakfast offer at 5:00 a.m. and had insisted they leave by six.

"You don't know how early they'll get there. I want to be there no later than seven a.m. Step on it, Sam."

Sam happily obliged. He liked driving Lisa's car, though it seemed small compared to his Lincoln. Lisa typed furiously on her laptop. That was her usual mode of work. Although she was frowning, he knew she was happy to be working.

They arrived at 6:50. They drove around the huge research facility to the truck docks in the back.

"Park someplace inconspicuous."

"Let's see. We can park here out of sight, behind the truck dock, and watch from the fence."

"Too conspicuous. Let's hide behind that evergreen."

"OK."

Sam and Lisa peeked through the juniper branches at the truck docks. In about fifteen minutes, an Illinois Best Disposal Truck backed up to the dock. A grain shoot moved over it and filled the truck bed.

"Got that, Sam?"

"All on video."

"Follow that truck," Lisa said as the truck pulled away.

"On it. I wonder where they're going to dispose of that grain? They've got to be in Midley soon."

"That's why we're watching them. I don't trust them any farther than I can throw that truck."

After traveling north on Route 51 for a while, the truck pulled into a small town. It turned into a farmhouse driveway. Sam drove past so as not to arouse their suspicions.

"Can you watch it, Lisa?"

Lisa pivoted around in her seat, holding her phone. "I'm watching and got it on video. It's going into a barn."

"Good. Let's stop and get some gas and a couple of apple fritters."

"Just a plain doughnut for me, Sam. I'm on a diet."

"Uh, OK." Lisa was thin. He was the one who could stand to lose a pound or two. Not that he wanted to, if it meant giving up apple fritters.

Sam came back with his apple fritter, two plain cake doughnuts, and two coffees.

"Hurry! They're pulling out." Lisa had the window open in the cold air, videoing the barn down the road.

"Got it. Let me put these down." Sam rolled to the driveway and watched the truck head north on 51. There was something wrong with it. It was a Corn-All truck now.

Sam grunted. "Huh. That was the truck that came out of the barn?"

"Yes. You saw the branding change?"

"Was that two trucks?"

"No, I think that had magnetic signage over the Corn-All trucks."

"I'm sure Corn-All wouldn't like that."

"That's not the least of what I think they're doing." Lisa smiled smugly.

"What else?"

"Just follow them discreetly."

"No problem. It's easy to be discreet when you're eating a sweet treat."

"But can you be neat?"

"Not yeet."

Sam and Lisa liked to get into rhyming games in their conversations. It was part of Lisa's hidden silly side Sam loved.

He followed at a sedate fifty-five half a mile behind the Corn-All truck, chowing down his fritter. He gulped the coffee to wash it down.

"Ah. It looks like he's getting off at the next exit."

"Well, well. Guess what's there?" Lisa smiled wickedly at her phone.

"What?"

"A Corn-All plant. Where they make grits and other cereals."

"OK, let me get this straight. They're taking grain meant for disposal as their private company and then they rebrand their truck and deliver it to Corn-All?"

"How much do you want to bet Corn-All is paying them for both the disposal and the grain?"

"That's a sucker bet."

"Very good! You're learning. I have hope for you."

They videoed the Corn-All truck dumping its load of grain from a driveway into a field a quarter-mile down the road.

"Now are they going to go back to the barn and get their Illinois Best Disposal signage?" Lisa mused.

Sure enough, the truck headed back south on Route 51 and took the exit to the same small town. They pulled into the same gas station and recorded the truck's transformation back into Illinois Best Disposal. Sam ordered another fritter.

"No more sweets for me. Get me something nutritious, like a beef stick," Lisa said.

Back on Route 51 again, Sam followed the empty truck to I-74, then I-474, and off at Bartonville.

"That's the right way to Midley." Sam pulled onto Route 29 and stayed a couple of hundred yards behind the truck.

"They'll be there right on time. I'll give them points for punctuality, if not honesty."

The truck picked up the garbage bins around town and took off to the north. They followed it to an Illinois Waste Disposal site near Peoria.

"Wait in the drive, Sam. I want to interview the trucker after he comes out. I assume it's Mark Victor. You go up to him first, then take the camera as I grill him."

"Got it."

Sam slid out of the car. After the trucker passed through the gate, Sam waved him down.

"Hi. Do you have car trouble?"

"No, I'm Sam Melvin, and the *Midley Beacon* editor Lisa Melvin would like to interview you about life as a truck driver. We'll pay you well for the interview, a hundred bucks."

"Sure. It sounds like an easy hundred, and this is my last stop of the day." He climbed out of his truck.

"Great." Sam waved to Lisa. She came out holding the video camera and her tablet. She handed the camera to Sam, then gave Mark a clip-on microphone.

"Mr. Mark Victor?"

"You got it."

"Thanks for agreeing to this interview. Where did you go today?"

"I did a load for Corn-All and then this load for Midley."

"Is this a pretty normal day for you, doing two loads in a day?"

"Yeah. You want to get multiple short loads or one long one in each day."

"And do you always shift your truck brands from Illinois Best Disposal to Corn-All?"

"What?"

"Watch." Lisa played the two transformations while holding up her tablet for Mark. "Here you go into the barn as Illinois Best and come out as Corn-All. Then here you go in as Corn-All and come out as Illinois Best."

"I want my lawyer. Keep your hundred."

"Your lawyer won't save you, Mark Victor. One of my friends is the sheriff for Macon County, where your barn is. I'll tip him off if you leave here without giving me the whole story. He'll get a warrant and investigate that barn within an hour."

"Uh . . ." Mark stamped his feet and looked down in the cold. "What if I continue the interview?"

"That's what I like to hear. We'll get the whole story of your scam and report it in the *Midley Beacon,* but keep it anonymous. Then you can keep your company and work for Corn-All with no more scamming. And provide us tips when Corn-All wants to dispose of any other GMO grain."

"I guess that's better than jail."

"You're right it is."

Mark's square face looked grim and bitter through the interview. They had sold the GMO grain back to Corn-All instead of disposing of it. To cover it up, they took other disposal jobs as Illinois Best and switched back to Corn-All.

"So in summary, you got paid for disposing the GMO grain, you got paid for selling it, and you got paid for disposing another load. Right?"

"You got it."

"And you use your friend's barn to store your magnetic signage for the Corn-All trucks so you can use their trucks for your private business?"

"Right."

"Anything else you can think of to tell me? If I find out later, I'll expose you."

"Isn't that enough? That's all we thought of."

"Who's your partner?"

"Uh . . ."

"You might as well tell me. I already have the incorporation papers for Illinois Best. I'd stop at the barn first."

"Will Ahern. His dad owns the barn. I don't want to drag them into it. They've got nothing to do with our scam."

"What does Mr. Ahern do?"

"He drives a truck for Corn-All too."

"And is a partner with you in Illinois Best Disposal?"

"Yeah. He and I dreamed this up together."

"Very good. All right, here's a phone for you, Mr. Victor." Lisa handed him a phone from her purse.

"What for?"

"I want you to report to me the day before you pick up any grain disposal from Corn-All. Since they produced the grain that produced the zombie turkeys, I wouldn't put it past them to try something like that again. If it happens, I want the *Midley Beacon* to have the scoop."

"All right, I guess."

"Here's another one for Will Ahern." She handed him another phone. "When will you see him next?"

"I'll drive straight for Willy's bar in DeKalb after we're done here. We meet for beers every day after work."

"Great. You've been a great interview, Mr. Victor. Here's your hundred. Your information has stopped a scam."

"You're not reporting me to the police? Really?"

"No, you're more useful as an inside informant on Corn-All. Bye."

After Mark pulled away, Sam looked at Lisa. "You sure about all this? It doesn't seem quite legal to me. Isn't this blackmail?"

"How can it be blackmail if we're paying him? Don't worry, Sam. These guys are small fry to the police and Corn-All. Just closing the loop on the leak of the zombie turkey GMO grain should make Corn-All eternally grateful to us. And they don't have to be incarcerated at public expense—they've gone straight on their own. News organizations have informants all the time. And they pay them a lot more than we paid Mark Victor."

"I've got one more question."

"Of course. That's why you're a good reporter. And detective."

"Thanks. I didn't know you knew the Mason County sheriff. Who is that?"

"Oh that. That was a bluff. It worked, didn't it? And I got a call from Oprah. We're going to see her tomorrow with your zombie friend."

Chapter 10 – West Hollywood

As they drove home, Sam said, "Lisa, if we're leaving tomorrow, what about our trucking scam story?"

"We've got the video. That's the hard part. Now it just needs to be edited and the story written. You're driving. I'll get it done before we get home." Lisa's fingers flew over the laptop like a centipede on meth.

"What time are we leaving tomorrow?"

"Eight a.m. from the Peoria airport. I'm sending Dan Cosana to pick up Bryan and Doris from Keokuk earlier in the morning." Lisa's typing didn't pause as she answered absently.

"That's an hour each way. He'll have to leave at five thirty."

"Five. We have to allow time for them to get through airport security."

"Oh. I think Bryan and Doris are already up that early, but I feel sorry for Dan."

"Don't. We pay him plenty."

* * *

The next morning, Lisa looked at Sam eating his breakfast. "What's that crap?"

"Grits. This is the box that made Bryan a zombie. We think. I'm testing it."

"It looks like wallpaper paste."

"It's not bad with butter and bacon and maple syrup."

"I'm not sure I want you to be a zombie. It'd be a good story though."

They arrived at the airport and saw Doris and Bryan in the lobby.

Sam shook Bryan's hand. "Hi, Bryan. I see your blue eyes. Contacts again?"

"Yes. I'm blind as a bat without them."

"You're still a zombie, right?"

"Sure. I don't want to disappoint Oprah."

"You'll do just fine, Bryan," Doris said

"Thanks."

"How's the raw-meat deal working out with you two?" Lisa walked beside them through the small Peoria airport.

"Oh, I've gotten used to it, Lisa. It's not so bad. It sure saves on cooking time," Doris responded.

"I've even gotten her to eat steak tartare." Bryan chuckled as they walked to the gate.

"After I learned how to make it on the internet," Doris said.

"Steak tartare? Isn't that raw steak?" Sam gave his boarding pass to the attendant.

"More like pickled steak hamburger. You add spices and booze."

"The more booze the better, Doris." Bryan laughed as he stepped through the plane's entrance.

"Boy, these first-class seats are great!" Doris plopped into hers.

"One thing for sure, Oprah's got the money." Lisa sat next to her.

Sam and Bryan settled in their seats in the row across the aisle. Sam set his fedora in the storage bin.

"You guys were already interviewed by her, weren't you?" Doris asked Lisa.

"Yes. It gave a big boost to our *Midley Beacon* paper, and we got a lifetime supply of turkey from her."

"That's funny after you guys almost died in the turkey apocalypse."

"Most than once. Excuse me, Doris. I've got to check on how our big story is doing." Lisa poked at her tablet rapidly.

"What big story is that?"

"Oh, the origin of zombie humans. It turns out the truckers were scamming Corn-All. They were hired to dispose of the GMO corn, and then they sold it back to them and disposed of someone else's waste instead."

"That's terrible!"

"Yes. So the GMO corn got back into the human food stream, and your husband's love of corn grits led to his zombiism."

"Have there been any others?"

"Not so far that I know of. Sam's been trying to turn zombie by eating the corn grits, but all he's gotten is a little tummy."

"I didn't think that grits had that many calories."

"When you eat it heaping with butter, sausage, and maple syrup it does."

"Oh."

Sam ordered a breakfast of eggs and bacon from the flight attendant. "I've had no success in turning into a zombie from your corn grits, Bryan."

"I guess I was just lucky."

"Or unlucky."

"No, on the whole, I think it's been a blessing. I'm getting nearly twice as much work done, both with the cattle and around the house for Doris. I need less sleep too."

"Wow. Now I feel unlucky. This'll be good stuff for the Oprah interview."

"I can't see how she can make me interesting for TV, even with zombiism."

"It's surprising. Just be yourself. They'll edit things in and out, and it'll all look slick and professional. Even I was interesting."

"I'll just roll with whatever happens. That was fun, being picked up by your plane this morning."

"Yeah, I like bopping about in the *Midley Beacon* plane too. I'm surprised Lisa's still paying our pilot, Dan. She's been on a cost-cutting kick."

"I heard that, Sam," Lisa chimed. "I've kept Dan Cosana on the payroll because it's still cheaper to pay him than to buy airline tickets."

"Oh. OK. Thanks, Lisa."

* * *

After lunch at LAX with the OWN representatives who'd met them at the airport, they rode to OWN's West Hollywood studio in a stretch limo.

Oprah greeted them as they came in. "Sam, Lisa! It's good to see you again." She embraced Sam and Lisa, then turned to the other couple. "You must be Bryan and Doris." She shook their hands. "Thank you for coming to my show."

"I used to watch it all the time when it was on broadcast TV," Doris said.

"Do you watch my OWN network?"

"No, we don't get cable. Maybe we will now!"

"I've moved on from broadcast TV to my OWN network. Now I only do special shows that I really want, like the first human zombie and his wife." She looked at Bryan's blue eyes and frowned. "Aren't you supposed to have red eyes?"

"I do. I just wear blue contacts." He popped one out and looked at her redly, glowingly.

"Ooo! We've got to have you do that during the show. Do you mind?"

"No, not at all. You've given us a free vacation here. It's the least I can do."

"You're giving me a chance to interview the first and only human zombie. I'm in your debt."

"OK, let's argue about it!" Bryan laughed, and Oprah joined him.

"I'll leave you with my producer, Julie Simpson, and she'll go over the show with you. Then we'll get you made up before we record it."

"Sounds good."

"See you in an hour, Bryan and Doris."

* * *

"You two look great!"

"Thanks, Lisa. I agree about Doris—her new hairdo and makeup are fantastic. For me, I just feel silly. I've never been powdered before."

"You look rugged and handsome. There's no visible makeup. If I wasn't sure of your love, I'd worry about some starlet grabbing you." Doris kissed his cheek.

"Thanks, Doris. I'm all yours, whether made up or not."

"You guys are making me all mushy," Lisa said.

"Here comes Oprah." Sam pointed as she entered the green room.

"Hi, guys! Doris, you look fabulous. Bryan, you're looking good too. I'll just ask you to tell your story about how you became a zombie. Doris, I'll ask you what it's like being married to a zombie. Do you want to practice your stories?"

"No, I'm good, thanks. Doris?"

"I'm good too, Oprah."

"All right. Our green room attendant, Aiden, will direct you to the stage when it's time." She nodded to a smiling young man. "Sam, Lisa, it's time to get into the audience."

"Will do." Sam nodded at her.

"Will you need anything from us, Oprah?" Lisa glanced at Oprah.

"No, just follow the directions of the stage manager for the audience."

* * *

"And that's a wrap. Thanks, everyone, for coming." The stage manager directed the audience to the studio exits.

"That went fast, and I wasn't even on stage, Lisa." Sam walked with Lisa out to the lobby, where they'd meet Bryan and Doris.

"It was annoying having to clap and cheer on cue."

"You just don't like anyone telling you what to do."

"True."

"Pretty diverse crowd." Sam watched the people walking by them: old, young, black, white, Hispanic, Asian, and some he couldn't recognize.

"That's what Oprah champions."

"And now zombies too."

"Why not? They're people too."

"Well, sure. And here they are. Hi, Bryan, Doris!"

"Hi, Sam. How did we do?" Doris looked anxiously at them.

"You were just fine," Sam reassured her.

"I felt so nervous! I should have practiced."

"It didn't come across, other than you talked faster than usual."

"I wanted to get it over with. You were as calm as a cucumber, Bryan."

"I just forgot about the camera and focused on telling the story to Oprah."

"You both were great! Do you want to come over to my house for an after party?" Oprah asked.

"Of course we do!" Bryan said.

"Can we come? I hope you have more of those cookies." Sam looked hopeful.

"I assumed you would come. Of course we have cookies— they're my favorite too!"

* * *

The Corn-All CEO Chet Zimmerman frowned at the board of directors. "Do we even know which truckers screwed us over?" He gestured to the *Midley Beacon* story about the crooked truckers spread out on the massive table. The board of directors had called a special meeting to discuss legal action.

"Yes, our private investigators are sure it's the Illinois Best Disposal company. They're the ones that contracted with us to dispose of the GMO corn from our laboratory." The Corn-All legal counsel Thomas Bismark didn't even look at his investigators' report in front of him. His dark-brown eyes peered directly into Chet's gray ones.

"But if we sue them, will it hold up in court? Will it even do any good? They don't have much money, do they? It just seems like a big waste of money." Chet grimaced, twisting his usually pleasant, bland face.

"We will definitely win. That'll remove the last stain or vestige of blame for the zombie disease from Corn-All and all liability. That's worth quite a bit of money, even if we get nothing from their liquidated assets."

"But will this flip around on us, publicity-wise? We're the big, mean corporation picking on poor, independent truckers."

"Not if we frame it as a crusade for justice against the evil zombie virus spreaders. I'm sure we can deliver that message to all the media outlets," Hannah Philodendron, the vice president of public relations, pointed out.

"Hmmm. We're damned if we do and damned if we don't. Let's get out from under the legal liabilities of this stupid GMO variant. That alone will be worth the money. Hannah, not only do we want to be crusaders against the evil zombie virus, but we want to be a zealous corporate neighbor helping those who've been affected. Even as we clear our name, let's step up our charitable giving to zombie widows and other people who've been affected. This way we'll be truly altruistic, since we're innocent of causing this disaster."

"Good idea, Chet." Hannah nodded, as did the rest of the board of directors.

"I take it we're unanimous about this course of action? All in favor say *aye*."

"Aye!"

* * *

As soon as they landed back in Peoria, Lisa's phone rang.

"Yeah? I know it's you, Mark. I've got caller ID. Why are you calling?" She grimaced.

"That could be bad. Let me consult my legal counsel. I'll call you back."

"What's up, Lisa?"

"It's Mark Victor, the crooked trucker we co-opted. Corn-All is suing him and his company for a hundred million dollars in damages."

"Oh no! They'll be ruined."

"Yeah, but that's not the problem. It'll probably wreck the *Midley Beacon* too, for aiding and abetting them."

"But we exposed their scam! At our own expense!"

"But we didn't turn them into the police. Sam, the first thing you need to know about lawsuits is that right and wrong don't matter—it's who has the most money who wins. And Corn-All has the most money."

"And they have been wronged by Illinois Best Waste Disposal. Who are you calling?" Sam had to hurry to keep up with Lisa through the parking lot.

"Slate Slatley. This'll cost the *Midley Beacon*. There go your chances of being hired back this month."

"Oh. I didn't know that'd happen."

"Well, you were generating enough money through your detective work that we could afford you a meager salary. Now, all that'll go to Slate. Hi, Slate. I need you. . . . OK, not over the phone. . . . We'll meet you there today. Bye."

Sam opened the door of his Lincoln for Lisa and then slid behind the wheel. "Where will we meet Slate?"

"Downtown Peoria in fifteen minutes. You still got a heavy foot?"

"The heaviest!" Sam drove around the airport road at fifty miles per hour and then sped up as he steered toward the freeway. Once there, the sky was the limit for him. He liked to break one hundred miles per hour on the I-474. Too bad they only had to go one exit.

They walked into the luxurious lobby of Slate Slatley's law firm in a skyscraper in downtown Peoria right on time.

Slate's secretary, Ms. Lucinda Lascovia, greeted them. "Mr. Slatley is expecting you. Please go right in." She gestured toward a door.

Slate, impeccably attired in a light-gray suit, stood. "Lisa, you never call me unless it's critically important. You have the rest of my day at your disposal."

Lisa made a moue, then sighed. "I don't want to spend a day of your time, but this may take that or more."

"Please explain everything from the beginning."

Lisa succinctly explained the truckers' scam of Corn-All and how she and Sam had exposed it and published it, hiding the names and company.

"High-risk behavior. If you could discover them, so could Corn-All."

"Right. It's my first big mistake of the year. And Corn-All is suing them."

"Is there anything in your article they could have used?"

Lisa was about to answer, when Sam said, "Sure. They know all the truckers they contracted and who carried away their GMO corn."

"I didn't think they'd bother."

"Having someone concrete to sue and assign responsibility removes all stain from Corn-All's reputation. They'd pay a lot to do that," Slate said.

"Yech. So how do I create a firewall between the truckers and us so we don't get caught up in the blame game?"

"Hmm. The truckers could stonewall, since unlike you, Corn-All doesn't have clear evidence of their malfeasance. But most likely, Corn-All will subpoena your evidence."

"I won't give it up!"

"You don't have to shout. I suppose you could destroy it, but that'd be a crime. So would withholding evidence. I think you're stuck."

"Can't we negotiate something with Corn-All?"

"What do you have to offer them? They'll want complete exoneration from the zombie plague—turkey, squirrel, cow, and human."

"How about if I endorse their products?" Sam said.

"What?" For the first time that Sam remembered, Slate Slatley looked startled. His mouth gaped in his normal poker face.

"I've been eating a ton of their corn grits, and I've grown to like them. How about I endorse their products as safe and non-zombie producing."

"That . . . might . . . work. They may go for it."

"How about we throw in free advertising on the *Midley Beacon*?" Lisa said.

Sam's jaw dropped. "You must be desperate. I've never heard you ever offer anything free before."

"You're right. But saying is, any publicity is good publicity. Good idea about the endorsements, by the way."

"Thanks. You made my day."

"I know."

Slate leaned back in his leather chair, steepled his hands in front of his chest, and looked at the ceiling. "That may be enough to close the deal. Let's see. You want to protect your sources, and you want to help Corn-All exonerate itself, right?"

"Yes."

"I'll draw up a contract. If you agree to it, I'll approach them about settling out of court."

* * *

Lisa, Sam, and Slate met the Corn-All lawyers in their office in Chicago at 9:00 a.m. the next morning. Sam and Lisa had driven up the night before. They'd enjoyed a night on the town before connubial bliss.

Three Corn-All lawyers met them in conference room 1B. A stocky black man stood. "Mr. and Mrs. Melvin? Mr. Slatley? I am Sam Smithers of Smithers, Smithers, and Smithers Limited. Allow me to introduce my colleagues, Stan Smithers"—a tall, thin man with brown hair nodded but didn't rise. "And Sue Smithers"—a round-faced, short woman nodded as well.

"All Smithers? Are you related?" Sam asked.

"No. We often get asked that despite our physical differences. We became friends in law school because of our last name and formed a law firm afterward. We work exclusively for Corn-All," Mr. Smithers said.

"Mr. Slatley, we have examined the proposal you emailed, and we believe we can work out an agreement."

Slate maintained his poker face and said nothing.

"In our counterproposal, we retain Mr. Melvin's services for ten years and the *Midley Beacon*'s for twenty. For gratis, of course."

"Why that's—" Lisa spluttered.

"Shhh, Lisa. I've got this." Slate took the counterproposal, read it slowly, and then pulled up his calculator app. He punched in numbers and wrote them down. He steepled his hands on the table and looked at Smithers, Smithers, and Smithers.

"According to my calculations, the value of twenty years of free advertising at the *Midley Beacon* is over two hundred million dollars, in 2016 dollars. That's assuming a two percent inflation rate and circulation of one million copies daily and a hundred million YouTube views daily."

"You've got to be—" Sue Smithers began.

Unperturbed, Slate continued. "Mr. Melvin's services, at his going rate, are worth forty million dollars over ten years, computed the same way. That net present value of two hundred and forty million dollars exceeds your lawsuit value by one hundred and forty million. You may resolve the difference by writing a check for that sum now."

Seeing their gaping mouths, Slate continued. "Alternatively, you can reduce the time of the settlement by sixty percent, which is the value difference between what you asked and what it's worth. That would be four years of promotion by Sam and eight years by the *Midley Beacon*. Finally, any combination of time reduction and money paid would be acceptable to my clients." Slate pushed a printout of his calculations to Stan Smithers, then sat back in his chair, with his hands folded, staring at the Smithers.

Stan frowned and looked at the calculations, then asked Slate, "Sam gets paid two thousand a day?"

"Currently. That is the lowest estimate I can give you. He is currently engaged by a billionaire who is recommending his services to other billionaires. A more accurate estimate would be his fees would increase to ten times that amount. I try to leave something on the table for you to take to Corn-All."

"Kind of you," Stan said, with no expression.

"The *Midley Beacon* really has a million daily subscribers?" Sue looked at Lisa, but Slate answered.

"Currently. Their circulation has increased fifty percent since the beginning of the month, as well as their YouTube views and subscribers. Those are separate groups of people."

"We will give your counterproposal due consideration and respond by the end of the day. This meeting is over." Stan stood.

They all shook hands, and the Melvins and Slate left.

"Wow. What do you think they'll do, Slate?" Sam asked.

"Not here. Wait until we get to the car."

Scooting into the Lincoln, Sam repeated his question. Slate sat in the backseat, although his Mercedes was also in the garage.

"Most likely they will accept the proposal, with small modifications that won't matter. I gave them enough to sell this to Corn-All."

"Clever of you to use Sam's highest fee rate as his base, as well as our highest subscriptions and YouTube hits," Lisa said.

"Basic negotiations You present the truth in the most favorable light."

"I still admire a master at work." Lisa smiled at him. "Let's do lunch."

"It's only ten o'clock," Sam noted.

"Then we call it brunch. This is my pre-celebration. I have a good feeling about this."

* * *

"Mr. Melvin, recording begins in one minute. Are you ready?"

"Sure. I'm always ready to eat Corn-All grits."

"Excellent." The video producer, Lil Zambonie, smiled and walked off the set. Sam glanced around the kitchen set: table, chair, counter, a bowl of hot grits before him, liberally laced with his favorite additive, maple syrup.

Lil signaled with her hand. The camera light turned red. Sam gave his famous smile.

"Hi! I'm Sam Melvin, the zombie detective. I can handle any zombie as long as I have my bowl of Corn-All grits first thing in the morning."

Sam paused and took a big spoonful and gulped it down.

"Delicious! And I personally guarantee you'll stay zombie-free. Now, you'll have to excuse me while I finish my bowl of Corn-All grits." Sam looked down at his bowl and took another enthusiastic spoonful.

"Cut!" Lil smiled. "That was great Sam. One take. You're a natural."

They took away his bowl of grits, and Sam felt disappointed. "I don't get to finish?"

"That was the commercial for the grits. Next, we have Sweet Corn Puffs. Then Corn-All Flakes, and finally Corn-All Ohs. I don't think you'll be lacking for breakfast this morning."

"Bring it on!"

* * *

"Sam, this lawsuit was a blessing in disguise!" Lisa told him after he came back to their Chicago hotel room from the recording studio.

"You're telling me! I actually got full from breakfast for once."

"Not that, silly man. I mean just the story from the lawsuit settlement has increased the *Midley Beacon*'s circulation and advertising revenue. I'm sure your commercials for Corn-All will increase your business."

"It's already picking up. I'm having to turn people down because I don't have enough time for them all."

"Raise your rates."

"I'm already charging twenty-five hundred a day!"

"Charge thirty-five hundred. How much competition do you have?"

"Um, none?"

"Right. Thirty-five hundred this month and more next month. You're the go-to detective for billionaires."

"Oh, and there's one more benefit for us."

"What's that?"

"Just before I left, Lil said I have a lifetime supply of Corn-All grits."

"Goody."

Chapter 11 – Criminal

The first call of the morning rang at 8:02 a.m.

"Hello, Sam Melvin, Zombie Detective."

"Hello, Mr. Melvin. This is Gary Howell, superintendent of police for Chicago."

"Wow. To what do I owe this honor, Superintendent?"

"You can just call me Gary. We need your expertise. We think we have a criminal zombie in Chicago."

"Oh. That could be bad."

"It is. We've caught him on security a camera doing smash-and-grab robberies from cars and stores. One of our officers shot him, but he just ran away. That's happened nine times so far."

"So you want my help catching him?"

"Yes. The mayor has already approved hiring you."

"When can we meet?"

"Today, if you want."

"I'll be there this afternoon. Where should I meet you?"

"At our headquarters on 3510 South Michigan Ave."

"I'll be there this afternoon."

"Great. Come right to my office."

* * *

Sam walked into the office in Chicago Police Headquarters. "Superintendent Howell?"

"Yes. Please call me Gary, Sam." A big smile creased his brown face below his glasses and bald head.

"Sure, Gary."

"I've prepared a briefing for you. Here are the videos in time order." Superintendent Howell pushed a button on his computer, and a wall-sized screen lit up, playing a black-and-white security video. A man wearing a ski mask punched a car window, opened the door, and took out a computer bag and a cell phone.

"That was the first crime. Here's the next." The same man knocked out a store's plate-glass window and grabbed a television.

Sam watched all twelve videos with Gary Howell. They all happened late at night, all the break-ins done by the man's fist. In the last video, taken from a policeman's body camera, the man was shot, and he stumbled but kept running and vaulted over a six-foot barbed-wire fence, clearing it with a foot to spare.

"Whoa! I can see why zombiism is suspect number one."

"Yes. We never found the bullets that were shot, and our video analysis show the man was hit in the leg and the back."

"And then did the Olympic high-jump stunt."

"Yes. We also analyzed his speed before the jump. Thirty miles per hour."

"So an Olympic sprinter as well as a jumper. Have you interviewed any decathletes in Chicago?"

Gary chuckled. "No. If he'd use his skills for good, he'd earn more than these smash-and-grab antics."

"Isn't that always the case with criminals? So where is all this happening?"

"Here on the south side of Chicago, in the baddest part of town." The superintendent brought up a map of West Fifty-First Street to West Seventy-Ninth Street and South Pulaski Road to I-90.

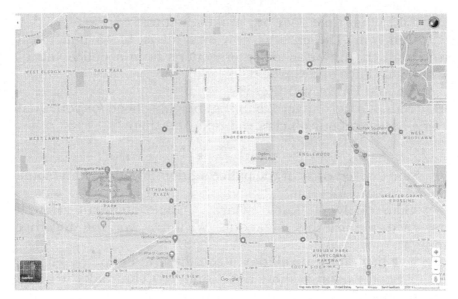

"Notice how he's avoiding West Engelwood. We think his base is there, in one of the abandoned buildings. He goes to parking lots or commercial areas around there, usually a block away."

"So it seems we should do a stakeout."

"Yes. That's what we have planned for tonight. But there's a problem."

"How do you catch a zombie? That's where I come in."

"Right."

"First, try putting rock salt in your shotgun charges."

"Because—oh, it kills the zombie bacteria. Right."

"I hope. It took a long time to dezombify a bull. Also, get a tranquilizer gun or two."

"To tranquilize him?"

"No, to shoot a syringe of salt water."

"I get it."

"But he still can run away."

"We can set up nets by the nearest streets to catch him."

"It's worth a try. Can we shoot a tracking device into him or on him?"

"Hmmm. We have GPS bracelets and anklets, but I can't imagine him staying still for us to put them on."

"Could we shoot one into him?"

"We do have tracking microchips. I'll have to ask if we can rig one up to be implanted by syringe or something."

"OK. What time does our stakeout start?"

"Ten p.m. The earliest he's ever hit is 11:45 p.m. We'll watch all the un-attacked intersections from a police van at West Fifty-Fifth and Garfield."

"Should I meet you there?"

"Nah. It's too dangerous in that neighborhood for you. Just come here, and our officers will take you there."

* * *

Sam arrived early at the police station. A young, handsome police captain met him.

"Sam Melvin? Lucio Garza. Superintendent Howell assigned me to this stakeout. We'll be working together tonight."

"I've been nervous all day. I couldn't even nap."

"I hope this is a short night and you can make it home before dawn."

"Probably not. I'll need to write up my daily case report for my business. I then copy that for the *Midley Beacon* to publish."

"So you have paperwork like I do? I had to get permits for the nets to be set in the escape paths."

"Oh? Where will they be?"

"Here's the map of the area."

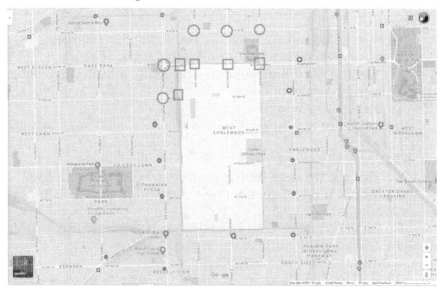

"Yes. Superintendent Howell showed me this afternoon."

"This is the map my men and I prepared about this suspect's activities. We have nets prepared at the intersections in squares. We'll be watching the intersections in the circles."

"Wow. This is a big operation."

"Yes. I have great hopes we'll get this guy, with your help. All my men have shotguns loaded with rock salt and tranquilizer guns."

"I'm eager to get him too."

"Let's get down to the squad car. We'll go there now"

* * *

They parked in Sherman Park, north of West Engelwood. The police van had ten monitors watching all the intersections and escape routes.

Sam was too nervous to sleep at first, but by midnight his head was nodding.

"Take a nap, Sam," Captain Garza said. "If anything happens, I'll let you know."

"Thanks. I'll just rest my eyes." Sam slid his fedora over his face and instantly fell asleep.

"Sam! There he is!"

Sam was sure he'd only been asleep for five minutes, but the clock on the monitor showed 1:46 a.m. The camera showed a man grabbing a computer bag, purse, and cell phone from a parked car.

"That's him?"

"Yes. About six feet tall, a hundred and eighty or so."

"Which intersection is that?"

"West Fifty-Fifth and Western Avenue. Uh-oh."

"What?"

"He's headed toward West Engelwood, but not toward our nets." Captain Garza clicked his radio. "Activate Australian Cattle Dog."

"What's that for?"

"We'll herd him into the nets with our squad cars."

A squad car sped down West Garfield next to them. Captain Garza shifted a monitor to a map of the area. Red dots showed four squad cars converging.

The camera showed the man dash down a side street. With squealing tires, a police car followed him. Another came from the other direction. More squealing sounded over the radio.

"He's doubled back to Garfield."

"We've got him in sight," said a policeman from another squad car.

Sam could see the criminal, holding the computer bag and purse, look up and down Garfield at the two approaching squad cars. He ducked down a street into West Engelwood—directly into their trap.

One net exploded from a trash can next to a building and covered the suspect. Another popped from the opposite side of the street from a transformer, trapping him in a double layer of netting.

"Great. Let's go pick him up." Captain Garza sped toward him.

"This seems almost too easy."

"It worked exactly as planned. That doesn't usually happen."

"You probably want to shoot him before you release him from the nets."

"We'll handcuff him first. That'll keep him under control. The city discourages shooting unless an officer's life is threatened."

They arrived and saw the man thrashing violently under the nets. He entangled himself more and more until it looked like he was in a ball of string. Sam and Captain Garza walked up to the grunting, fighting zombie.

He stopped and looked at them with glowing red eyes. "You're Sam Melvin! I recognize your hat. I saw you on Oprah."

"Yes, that's me."

"Give up quietly, and it'll go easier for you," Captain Garza said.

The zombie glared at Sam. "You're behind this trap—I know it. I'll get you!" He put his hands together in one loop of the netting and tore it. PONG! PONG! The nylon cords snapped like violin strings.

"He's getting away! Use the tranquilizer guns!"

PUMPF! PUMPF! PUMPF! Three muffled shots preceded three syringes sticking into the man's chest. He stopped his net tearing to pull them out.

"You'll never catch me!" With a final tear, he leapt out of the nets and jumped up to the second-story windowsill on the nearest building. Quickly, he climbed to the roof and then jumped off on the other side.

"Get the helicopter over here to look for him," Captain Garza ordered.

The helicopter, waiting quietly in Sherman Park, zoomed into the air, looking for the suspect.

They didn't find him.

* * *

"Well, that didn't work." Superintendent Howell began the meeting. He'd met Sam and his officers in the debriefing room in the police headquarters early that morning.

"No. And everything went right. And he still got away," Captain Garza said.

"Got any ideas, Sam?"

"Yes. As I mentioned last night, you needed to shoot him while he was still in the nets."

"We did! We hit him three times."

"But he pulled out the syringes before they'd emptied their salt water. Try shotguns with rock salt next time. It's hard to pull out hundreds of salt crystals."

"That's a problem. That's against Chicago police rules of engagement. You must try nonlethal methods of arrest first."

"Salt pellets are nonlethal to zombies. Heck, shotguns, pistols, and rifles are nonlethal. I've seen turkeys come back from all of those, and a person is a lot bigger and stronger than a turkey."

"I'll talk to the mayor and the city council and see if I can get an exception in this case."

* * *

Sam propped his shotgun up in his Chicago hotel room. Chicago had clamped down on guns again since the end of the zombie turkey plague, and it would have looked suspicious if he carried it around openly. So he stored it in a trombone case he'd bought at a pawn shop in Peoria.

He'd gotten his conceal and carry license back during the turkey apocalypse, and that worked perfectly with his new career as a private investigator.

He typed up his case report for the day and then sent a copy to Lisa. She'd rewrite it and publish it in the *Midley Beacon*.

He yawned. Boy was he tired! The bedside clock showed 10:00 a.m., so he'd been awake for thirty hours. Time for some shut-eye.

He set the alarm for four o'clock. He needed to shower and have supper before another night staking out this zombie. Despite the sun streaming in the window, he fell asleep immediately.

And woke just as quickly. Someone was pounding his door.

"Sam Melvin! Sam Melvin! I need to speak to you!"

Blearily, he saw the time was one o'clock. *Who could it be? Not the cleaning crew.*

He opened the door with the chain on. It was still Chicago. Sam saw a man with dark eyes, dark, scruffy hair, and three days of beard.

"Yes? What do you want?"

"You're Sam Melvin?"

"Yes."

BAM! The man smashed his fist into the door, breaking the chain and throwing Sam backward. He stumbled into his bed.

"I want you, Sam Melvin! You're ruining my life!" He stalked toward Sam on the bed.

"What have I ever done to you?"

"You tipped off the police, and I nearly got caught."

"Wait. Are you that zombie criminal?"

"What do you think?" He picked up Sam, smashed him into the ceiling, and dropped him.

Sam fell half on the bed and flopped to the floor. His hand touched his shotgun.

"Ha!" Sam swung it toward the zombie and pulled the trigger.

Nothing happened. The safety was on.

As he fumbled it off, the criminal tore it out of his hands and tossed it out the window. The glass shattered, and the gun banged off the frame and fell with a clatter. The glass tinkled as it descended twenty stories.

Sam's heart sank. His last hope was two hundred feet away.

"Now it's your turn." He picked Sam up to throw him out the window.

"Why?"

"I finally made it as a criminal when I became a zombie, and now the whole police department is after me!" He hurled Sam toward the broken window.

His aim was perfect, throwing Sam right toward the middle of the gaping window. Sam couldn't avoid the window frame that bisected it. He caught it with his hands and stomach. His torso went out the window on one side, and his legs on the other. Good! He wouldn't fall—then the aluminum frame broke at the bottom, not strong enough to hold his weight.

Sam clung to the slender vertical slat for dear life as he fell heavily on the nine-inch-wide ledge outside. He tore his eyes off the drop below and saw the horizontal frame buckle where it joined the vertical one, saving Sam's life.

"Drop and die already!" The crazed zombie charged the window.

Of all things, Sam noticed his butt was profoundly uncomfortable. He shifted his hips and found he was sitting on the shotgun. Without thinking, he grabbed it and pointed it at the zombie, just as he hit his aluminum lifeline with his fist.

Everything happened at once. The frame came off in his left hand. Holding the gun upright in his other hand, he accidentally pulled the trigger, without aiming. The recoil of the gun tore it from his hand and slammed it into the window ledge, where it bounced and cartwheeled downward.

Sam slipped off the ledge. Convulsively he hurled himself backward and grabbed—something in each hand. His attacker's ankles.

Sam's eyes zoomed in on the criminal leaning out the window. He covered his face with both his hands after taking the shotgun blast there. His blood dripped on Sam's legs, dangling down.

Pulling the criminal's ankles with all his might, Sam dragged his body over the broken glass and through the window.

Lying on his back between a murderous zombie's ankles didn't seem like the safest place, but at least he was alive. The zombie's ankles flexed, and Sam let go. Still holding his bleeding face, the zombie tilted forward and fell.

Sam couldn't help himself. He sat up to watch the fall, with his calves still hanging out the window. End over end the man fell, seemingly unconscious. He landed partly on the sidewalk, partly on the curb. There was no big splat, just a crumpled body far below.

Sam crawled back to his bed, picked up his cell, and dialed Superintendent Howell.

"Sam? I'm in a meeting. Can you call me back?"

"Uh, yes. But I got the zombie."

"What? How? Where?"

"He's lying on the sidewalk by Capone's Hotel, where I'm staying. He fell twenty stories."

"How'd you do that?"

"I shot him as he was throwing me out the window."

"We'll be right there." He hung up.

"Uh. Now what?" Sitting on the floor, Sam looked at his wrecked room. Cold winter air blew in his window and out the broken door. His head ached from where he'd banged into the ceiling. His pajamas were torn and bloody. He was still sleepy.

His phone rang. A video call.

"Sam, why the hell haven't you called?" Lisa's expression changed from ferocious to curious. "Oh, you look like crap. What happened?"

"Uh, I caught the zombie—or he caught me."

"Don't worry. I control the narrative. Now give me the complete report. I'm recording this."

Sam relayed his afternoon's activities.

"Well. It's a good thing you survived. I'd have killed you if you died on me."

"Uh, thanks?"

"This, of course, will be front-page news across the country. Twirl in front of the camera. I want to see how bad your injuries are."

"If I can stand." Sam propped the phone against the clock radio and then, with a grunt, heaved himself upright. He was cold in his pajamas with the frigid air. He turned in front of the camera.

"Good, good, plenty of blood. I'll take a couple of stills of this video for the article. Maybe I can post this on YouTube?" Lisa asked herself.

"Lisa, I need to get dressed. I'm freezing."

"OK. You sound a lot better. Check in with a doctor. Some of those cuts might get infected."

"The police'll be here in a few minutes. I hear the sirens now."

"Put your phone video on record. I don't want to miss anything."

"All right."

"Sam, I do love you. Keep up the great work!"

"Thanks, Lisa."

Soon after Sam finished dressing, Superintendent Howell walked in with Captain Garza.

"Sam! Are you OK?"

"I think so. I need to see a doctor."

"Come with me. We'll go right to the police doctor. He's down looking at our zombie."

"Not a job I'd like."

"Someone's gotta do it."

* * *

The police doctor looked up from the body as Sam and the others approached. He looked grim.

"I've done all I can. He's barely alive."

Sam stopped short, his headache and cuts forgotten. "Alive? He fell twenty stories. I was sure he was dead."

"Fewer bones are broken than you'd expect, and he doesn't appear to have internal injuries, amazingly."

"Sam fought him off before he fell," the superintendent said. "He's got some cuts and bruises. Could you check him out, Aaron?"

"Sure. Come into the ambulance for some privacy."

Dr. Aaron Bilco examined Sam's head and cuts. He picked out some pieces of glass, treated them with antibiotics, and gave Sam an aspirin for his headache.

"That's a nasty bruise on your head, but you don't seem to have a concussion or a fracture. Let's check again tomorrow to be sure."

Sam started to leave to work on his case report and then stopped. He had to find out about the zombie criminal. He turned back to Dr. Bilco.

"Say, could I talk with the guy who fell twenty stories?"

"We've got him in Northwestern hospital. He's recovering slowly. The last few broken bones are still going to be healing for months."

"I'd like to check with him to see how he is."

"Don't stay any longer than necessary. Here." The doctor signed a piece of paper and gave it to Sam.

"What's this? 'This man has permission to see this patient as long as the doctor or head nurse thinks it is prudent. Dr. A. Bilco, Chicago PD.' Ah, access."

"Right. Normally you wouldn't be allowed at all."

"Got it."

Sam walked to his car in the hotel garage and drove to the hospital. The head nurse scowled at his request, suspiciously scrutinized Dr. Bilco's note, and then said, "You've got five minutes. Starting now." She looked at her watch.

"Which room?"

"327."

Sam walked into the room. The man didn't seem so fearsome lying on the bed in a torso cast with an IV in his arm.

"You! Sam Melvin."

"Yeah. I thought I'd see how you're doing."

"Alive . . . and in pain. I've got some painkillers in me, but they don't seem to be enough."

"Could you ask for more?"

"Not needed. I can self-administer a dose when I want. I'm trying to see how far I can stretch it."

"Oh. I never found out your name."

"I guess it doesn't matter anymore. I'm Elmore Figaro, but just call me 'El.'"

"What made you go into crime?"

"Ha! Growing up in the hood, we always boosted stuff. I stole my first pair of shoes at six. After going through arrests and the JD home as a teen, I came back to the south side as a professional. I was a lot more careful. I only got arrested every couple of years or so. Then I became a zombie."

"How'd you become a zombie? When'd that happen?

"Maybe a week before now. I noticed I needed to sleep less, and then my landlady told me to check my eyes for pink eye."

"You don't happen to like grits, do you?"

"Yeah, how'd you know?"

"Lucky guess. So you became a zombie and resisted arrest. And then you got careless."

"You got that right. I felt invincible, especially after I survived getting shot. I saw the bullet come out of my leg as it healed. I didn't think the police would put the resources they did into my little thefts."

"But they did."

"And they got you, the smart-asses. I'd still be a zombie if it weren't for you."

"So you're not a zombie?"

"Would I be laid up like this if I were?"

"I guess—"

"Times up. Out you go, Mr. Melvin." The nurse interrupted their dialogue.

"Can I come back tomorrow, Nurse Richter?"

"Yes. For five minutes."

"See you, El. Get well!"

* * *

Back in his hotel room, Sam's head finally cleared up. He typed up the day's case report and was about to send it off to Lisa, when his phone rang.

"Hi, Oprah."

"Hi, Sam. I read that you captured a zombie today in the *Midley Beacon*. How are you feeling? You looked pretty beat up in the YouTube report."

"I've been better and I've been worse. I'm on the mend."

"That's good. I've got a favor to ask."

"What, another interview? This guy'll be in the hospital for months."

"Oh, that's too bad. Do you think you can get some of his blood for me?"

"I don't think that'll help. He's lost his zombie infection."

"Crap. I was hoping it would help me lose weight."

"Can't you call Bryan?"

"I already did. He went back to normal already."

"I'm sorry about that."

"I'm so desperate. I've started eating Corn-All grits."

"Ha! You know that never worked for me. Dr. Marchanne Herbst at the Mayo Clinic thinks it has something to do with my gut bacteria."

"Yeah, I've seen the commercials. Well, keep me in mind if you run into any other zombies. This is my private number."

"Will do, Oprah."

Chapter 12 – New York City

"Sam, this is Oliver Dirkse, NYPD chief detective."

Sam hurriedly washed his hands in the bathroom while holding his phone between his neck and cheek.

"Oh, ah, hi there, Detective." Sam dried his hands. He hadn't even had time to get to his desk this morning.

"Did I catch you at a bad time?"

"Ah, no, I'm good." Sam hustled to his home office and sat at his desk.

"Good. This is critically important. We have a murder case, and we suspect a zombie's involved."

"So you called me."

"Yes. I just read *Midley Beacon* about your successful apprehension of the criminal in Chicago yesterday, and I'm impressed."

"Thanks."

"So when can you get to New York City to help us?"

"Uh, I guess by tomorrow."

"That's good. I'll deposit your first week's pay in your online account."

"Thanks."

"I'll brief you tomorrow at eight a.m. at One Police Plaza in Manhattan."

"How do I get there?"

"Just ask your taxi driver to get you there."

"OK."

"See you tomorrow."

Sam immediately told Lisa, who was at her computer in her home office. "Lisa, I got another job."

"Great! What and where and how much?"

"It's a murder case in New York City. They suspect a zombie's involved. They already paid the first week."

"That's over twenty-one thousand! I bet it's another Corn-All grit-eating person. We should advertise for Corn-All. Oh, we already do. When do you have to leave?"

"I have to be there tomorrow by eight a.m."

"OK. I'll finish up the stories I have and drive you to the airport."

"Great!"

* * *

Sam settled into the grimy taxi in front of his Manhattan hotel.

"Where to, Mac?"

"One Police Plaza."

"Sure thing, bud." He flipped the meter on, and $6.50 appeared. He drove around the block, and it went to $7.00. Then he stopped.

"Here we are." He flipped the meter off.

"What? I could have walked here!"

"I s'pose. That'll be seven bucks."

Sam counted out seven dollars.

"What? No tip? I coulda driven ya all 'round New York b'fore droppin' ya off."

"Oh." Sam gave him another dollar bill.

"Piker." The driver slammed the door and drove off.

Sam walked into the police station. *Hmm. I remember telling the taxi driver from the airport last night to get me to a hotel near the police station. I guess he did his job. I'll have to check for walking distance from now on.*

Sam looked upward and stared at the red brick, upside-down, brutalist pyramid that was One Police Plaza. *That's different.* He tripped over a step and walked into the lobby, also lined with red brick.

The receptionist called Chief Detective Dirkse, and a young detective guided Sam to his office.

"Sam! It's good to see you in person. I've watched you and Lisa many times on YouTube. Welcome to the home of New York's finest." The bulky detective stood and shook Sam's hand. He was shorter than Sam's five ten but massively built, with his belly straining against his dress shirt.

"Thanks, Chief Dirkse. I heard you have a murder case."

"Yes. Let me brief you on the particulars. We received a 911 call a few days ago, complaining about screaming in an apartment next door. When the officers arrived, it was quiet. We entered the apartment in question and saw a man tear off the head of a woman. We shot him, but he jumped out of the window with the head and ran away."

"Ugh. That sounds like a zombie to me. Any motive? Who was this lady?"

"A madam of a brothel in Manhattan, Layla Longoria."

"Do you think he might have been a client?"

"That's one angle we're investigating. The sex workers are close mouthed about their customers. We got some pictures of the man from the police body cameras. Here's a picture we've been showing to all the girls." He handed over a black-and-white glossy.

"Hmmm." The photo showed a swarthy bearded man with a round object under his arm, looking directly at the camera. Sam realized that must be the head. *Yuck.* The bearded man's eyes seemed to glow.

"Did the officers notice if his eyes glowed red?"

"Yes. They both remarked on that, and it was captured in the photo. As well as the effect of the bullet."

"What? Oh." Sam reexamined the photo and saw a dark stain on the man's hoodie, near the belt. "So they plugged him in the stomach."

"Yes. And then several times in the back as he fled." Chief Dirkse handed over two more photos, one showing the man heading toward the window and one going through it. In the first photo, Sam saw a black spot on the back of the hoodie on the right side of the back. In the second, there was a second spot on the left side.

"So he took three bullets. What caliber of gun?"

"Nine millimeter Glock, our standard pistol."

Sam jabbed at the calculator app on his tablet. "That's about a thirty-five-and-a-half caliber. There's no way three bullets would stop a zombie human. They'd barely stop a turkey for a few minutes."

"So we saw. He also jumped from a third-story window and ran away."

"Yeah, that's nothing. The zombie guy in Chicago jumped twenty stories and would have recovered completely except for the rock salt in him. So I guess you need to equip your police with shotguns loaded with rock salt."

"OK, but first we have to find him. We can hide a million zombies in NYC. Got any tips on how zombies think?"

"Umm." Sam tried to remember all he could about Bryan and Elmore. "Mentally, they stay the same. Bryan stayed a cattle farmer. Elmore stayed a street thief. Physically, they're more active, stronger, more aggressive, and they need less sleep."

"I'll have you meet the detectives on the case." He pressed his comm. "Tammy? Send in Boxer and Poodles."

"Your detectives are named Boxer and Poodles?"

"Boxer is his real name. Ted Boxer. 'Poodles' is a nickname for Penelope Palmer."

"I'd think she'd go by 'Penny.'"

"She hates Penny. Don't ask her why. Wait till you see her."

The pair entered. Ted Boxer was a smiling, handsome man in his forties with short blond hair combed back from his forehead. Penelope, or Poodles, was half a head taller than Ted, with long legs and arms and curly hair englobing her head in a sphere of ringlets.

"Boxer, Poodles, this is Sam Melvin. I told you he'd be helping."

"Pleased to meet you, Sam." Ted pumped his hand vigorously.

"Likewise."

Sam looked to Poodles. She had an attractive brown face with a serious, almost stern look.

"I don't do glad-handing. I don't like people in general."

"Uh, OK. So I should call you Poodles?"

"That's my name." She looked reproachfully at Sam, like he should know better.

"Sam'll brief you on what he told me and answer any questions you have about zombies."

As Sam described zombies, Poodles interrupted him. "You say gunfire doesn't affect them?"

"No. They just heal and regenerate within minutes."

"Crap on a stick. How do we stop them?"

"Shotguns loaded with rock salt work, eventually."

"Eventually? What does that mean?" Poodles glared at him, apparently for his imprecision.

"With the zombie bull, it took twenty or thirty loads and about four hours. With Elmore, one shot in the face knocked him out, but it still took nearly half an hour."

"So we could blast this creep, and he'd still be able to kill us?"

"That's about it."

"We need better weapons, Chief." Poodles turned her ire toward Chief Dirkse.

"Sam? Do you have any suggestions?" Dirkse raised one eyebrow toward Sam.

"Flamethrowers are really effective on turkeys."

"Be realistic. How could we use that inside?" Boxer said.

"Uh, you probably can't. Steel cages work well."

"How about steel netting?"

"Good idea, Pen-uh—Poodles. They tried nylon nets in Chicago, and the guy Elmore tore them."

"Yeah, I read up on the case." Her face now showed some grudging respect toward Sam.

He felt better, like he'd passed some test. A strange thought crossed his mind. *How would Poodles and Lisa get along?* He felt they'd either love or hate each other.

"Sam?" Chief Dirkse prompted him. Apparently, someone had asked him something.

"Oops. I was woolgathering. What did you say?"

"Boxer here wondered if there was some remote weapon that would stop a zombie in its tracks, besides a flamethrower."

"Uh, a flamethrower doesn't really stop them quickly— turkeys I mean. They just run away. Let me think. Oh, I know."

"What?" Boxer and Poodles chorused and then looked at each other.

"Fléchettes. The army used them against the turkeys, and they shredded them. They had some that injected salt water."

"Hmmm. That's great for the army, but I don't think I can get those for the NYPD. I'm on a tight budget." Chief Dirkse looked frustrated.

Boxer's normally smiling face sagged. Poodles's brow furrowed in anger.

"Maybe I can help. How about if you borrow some? How many do you need?"

"Two?" Boxer said.

"Six," Poodles said.

"Let's ask for a dozen. But how can you get military gear?"

"Oh, I know a captain in Maryland and one in Illinois from the National Guard. I think I can call in a favor or two."

"How long will it take?" Poodles asked.

"Let me call them now." Sam speed-dialed Captain Carpenter. "Hi, Captain Carpenter. . . . I've got a favor to ask. . . . Could I borrow some of your saltwater fléchette guns? . . . It's for New York City police. They've got a zombie murderer on the loose. . . . That's real nice of you." Sam jotted down a number. "OK, I'll call him in an hour."

"Did you get the rifles?" Dirkse asked.

"Uh, no. Captain Carpenter can't loan them out of the state. But he knows the National Guard head in New York City, and he'll call him. He gave me the number too, to call him in an hour."

"Do you want me on the call?"

"It can't hurt, Chief. I'll come back here in an hour." Sam followed Boxer and Poodles to their office, a floor down.

"Are we just going to twiddle our thumbs for an hour? We've got work to do on this case."

"How about I work with you, Poodles? Boxer?"

"Sounds great!" Boxer said.

"OK. We were planning out our interviews of the other prostitutes in the brothel." Poodles pointed to white board.

"I've done a lot of interviews," Sam said.

There were three prostitutes on their list. They'd been notified they were material witnesses to the murder and on house arrest. They all lived in the same hotel as the murdered madam.

"Sam, the way we usually work is, I interview first and then Poodles. We have our standard interrogation questions. Let's review our questions with you."

"Who, what, where, why, when, and how. That's the reporter's mantra."

"Yes, that pretty much covers it, except for the details."

"So what are you going to do, Sam?" Poodles tipped her head to one side.

"I thought I'd just observe you two and suggest a question or two."

"Right. Let's do this."

* * *

As they slid out of the car parked down the street from the Elysian apartment building, Poodles shouldered the fléchette rifle. It took a .50 caliber shell and was long and heavy. They'd picked up three of the rifles from the NY National Guard after lunch.

"I like this." Poodles patted the rifle fondly.

Boxer walked quickly in front of them. "The first girl is Shawna Taylor. She's the one who called the police." Boxer led them into the apartment building and up the stairs. "Apartment 3G. Here's a floor layout, Sam."

Third Floor Layout

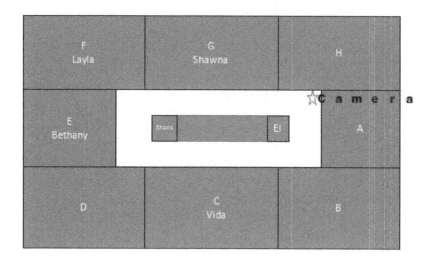

Sam noticed the building was clean and well maintained. *This is a brothel?* Boxer knocked on the door.

"Hello?" An attractive young lady peered through the door crack held by half a dozen chains.

"Ms. Shawna Taylor? We're from the NYPD. We have some questions for you about the murder of Layla Longoria."

"Oh. They told me to expect someone. Could I see your badges?"

Boxer and Poodles showed their badges. Sam showed his PI card.

"A private investigator from Illinois? That's weird. At least you've got a fedora." She unlocked her door and let them in.

The detectives sat on the living room couch, Sam on an armchair.

Shawna sat on the other armchair. "Shoot."

"How long have you known Layla?" Poodles asked calmly.

"I started working for her a year ago. She saw me working on the street and asked if I wanted to move up in the business."

"What did you witness two nights ago that caused you to call the police?" Boxer asked.

Sam looked at her heart-shaped face, the color of coffee with cream. *She's too good looking to be a prostitute.*

"First I heard yelling and screaming in Layla's apartment. She's right next door to me. When it grew louder, I went to her apartment door and listened, and then I peeped in. I saw the back of a man leaning over the couch. I heard Layla say, 'No!' And then there was nothing. The man looked around and saw me. He had bright-red eyes. I screamed and went into my apartment and called the police."

"This all happened when? What time?" Poodles looked at her with sympathy.

"Night before yesterday."

"February eleventh?"

"Yes."

"And what time?"

"The police got here really fast. It was twelve fifteen a.m. I saw the clock when I opened the door to them. So this happened probably at five to twelve."

"How long were you at the apartment door?" Poodles continued.

"No more than five minutes. Maybe three."

"Which apartment is it?"

"3F."

"Was this the man you saw?" Boxer handed her a photo of the murder suspect from the security camera.

"Yes!" She shivered, her long, curly hair shaking. "I hope I never see him again. Creeped me out totally."

"There was no other person in the apartment? Did you see Layla?" Boxer sounded surprised.

"No. I just heard her voice from behind the couch. No way in hell was I going in there!"

"Was there anyone else in your apartment or the hall?" Now Poodles spoke.

"No. My client had gone home. I was relaxing. The hall was empty. I don't know what the other girls were doing."

"Did the man speak to you all? Say anything?"

"No. Our eyes met for no more than a second before I ran to my apartment and locked my door."

"Did you hear a man's voice at all while you were outside?"

"No. I only heard Layla yelling and things crashing around."

"What did you do after running to your apartment and locking the door?" Poodles looked intently at Shawna.

"I immediately called the police."

"Nothing else?"

"Well, I did look for a new door lock and bought one while I waited. It's this one here." She rose and pointed to a shiny, massive lock on the doorjamb, below the others.

"And you didn't say anything to Layla or the man?"

"No! I was too scared."

"How did the man react when he saw you?"

"He just glared with those red eyes. That's all I remember."

"Did you report this to anyone else in the building? To the management? To the other girls?" Boxer took over for Poodles.

"No. Just the police."

"How about afterward? Did you tell anyone about the incident or behavior?"

"I tell you, I was so shaken, I stayed in my apartment except for getting the mail. I got the lock the next day and installed it. I didn't go out at all. I ate some Corn Flakes and leftover Chinese food."

"Do you know why the incident occurred?"

"I have no clue. Layla didn't have any enemies that I knew of. She made pretty good money off our business, so maybe he wanted her money."

"Do you know anyone else who can shed light on this incident?"

"I guess the other girls might have heard something. They might have been busy with clients. I don't know."

"Are they on this floor?"

"Yeah, we're all together. Bethany's in 3E, and Vida is around the corner in 3C."

"Is there anything else you want to tell me that I haven't asked you?" Boxer finished up.

"Uh, I can't think of anything."

"Sam, you got anything?"

"Uh, yeah. Shawna, before he turned around, he was leaning on the back of the couch like this?" Sam leaned over the back of her couch, between Boxer and Poodles.

"Yeah, that's it."

"Was he looking at the floor like this or the couch like this?" Sam shifted his glance from one spot to another.

"More like he was looking at the floor."

"And his hands were on the back of the couch like this?"

"Maybe a little farther apart. He wasn't really putting any weight on them."

"Thanks. That's all for now."

"Thank you, Shawna." Boxer shook her hand. "You've been a great help."

"If we have any more questions, we'll come back," Poodles added.

They closed the door and heard Shawna locking up.

"The next girl is Bethany. Apartment 3E."

They went around a corner. 3E was on the other side of 3F, which was a corner apartment. Police tape covered the door of 3F.

"So you've got it sealed off?" Sam studied the door.

"Yeah. The forensics team is done, but they might come back."

"Thanks, Poodles."

Boxer knocked on 3E. "Hello? Who is there?" sang a high musical voice.

"This is the NYPD."

"Oh. C'mon in, then." The door opened to a short blond girl with big blue eyes, plump and curvy, in jeans and a T-shirt.

"Ms. Bethany Miller?"

"Yes, that's me."

"We're here to interview you about what happened to Layla Longoria."

"Oh. Have a seat." She gestured toward a love seat and one armchair. Poodles and Boxer took the love seat and Sam the armchair. Bethany pulled a chair out of the kitchenette and perched on it.

"How long have you known Layla?" Poodles began.

"Over three years. She and I were working on Park Avenue when we met. She suggested starting our business, and we did."

"Were you co-owners of your sex firm?"

"I could have been, but I didn't want to do all the work of recruiting and accounting. And firing."

"What did you see and hear two nights ago?"

"Not much. I was busy with a client, and I couldn't stop. I heard some commotion out in the hall, but it soon died out."

"In the hall? You didn't hear anything from her apartment?"

"I wasn't really listening. And the bathroom and shower are between my apartment and hers. That blocks the noise."

"What did you hear?"

"Just some muffled yelling."

"Male or female?"

"I couldn't tell."

"Did you hear the police enter?" Boxer jumped in.

"No."

"What time did your client leave?"

"About one a.m."

"Then when did you leave the next morning?"

"Not until my usual time. I go out for lunch around noon."

"When did you find out what happened?"

"Shawna checked in on me the next morning, and I got the news."

"Were you surprised?" Poodles asked.

"Yes. It didn't seem real to me. It still doesn't."

"Was there anyone you know who wanted her dead?"

"Not really. There are a few other madams around the east side, but it's a friendly rivalry."

"Could you give us a list of those women?" asked Boxer in a warm, friendly voice.

"I guess so. I don't have a choice, do I?"

"This is not an arrest—it's an investigation. You don't have to cooperate. However, it's far more likely we'll find Layla's murderer the more you help us."

"There's nothing to stop him from killing me next, I suppose. Let me write down the ones I know." Bethany wrote on a pad of paper, tore off the sheet, and handed it to Boxer.

"Thank you. Have you seen this man before?" Boxer handed her a photo of the murderer.

She studied it. "No. I have a good memory of faces. Maybe one of the other girls will recognize him. He looks rough. Why are his eyes shining like that?"

"He's a zombie," Sam said.

"Ew. But he doesn't look like he's rotting."

"It's like the zombie turkey plague last year. The zombie disease regenerates body parts and makes the eyes glow."

"Huh. I hadn't heard it'd gone into humans."

"The first couple of human zombies showed up this month, in Keokuk and Chicago."

Bethany looked at Sam. "You're not with the NYPD, are you? You're not from New York."

"No, I'm a private investigator from Illinois. I specialize in zombies—and other odd things."

"Cool."

"Shawna talked with you. Did you hear from Vida?" Poodles asked in her cool, professional voice.

"No. She sleeps late, later than me."

"She didn't stop by?"

"Nope."

"What did you do last night? Did you have any clients?"

"No one was scheduled. With the police tape everywhere, I would have canceled them anyway. Some clients get nervous."

"So what did you do last night?"

"I just stayed home and watched Netflix. It was good to have a night off."

"When you found out about the murder, did you talk to anyone about it?" Boxer smoothly took over the interview.

"No. I was in shock most of the day, trying to think about our business and what we'd do without Layla. I don't want to manage it, but I might have to."

"Do you know why anyone might have wanted to murder Layla?"

"No, she's just a madam. She didn't hurt anyone. I don't get it."

"Can you think of anyone else who can shed light on this incident?"

"Hmmm. You've got those names. And you'll interview Vida and Shawna, right?" She looked at Boxer's nod. "Maybe you can check the other people on this floor?"

"We will, Bethany. Is there anything else you want to tell me that I haven't asked you?"

"Well, maybe I have a question for Sam. How dangerous are these zombies? I know a lot of people died from the zombie turkeys, but how bad are zombie humans?"

Sam shook his head. "Honestly, we don't know. This is just the third one I've found. Like the zombie turkeys, zombie humans are faster and stronger than normal humans. I'd guess they can get as bad as people can get."

"Now I'm really scared."

"That's why we're here, Bethany." Boxer spoke in his most comforting way, like a big brother talking to his sister. "We'll get him. Thank you, Bethany." Boxer shook her hand. "You've been a great help."

"Sam, do you have any questions?" Poodles looked at him and arched an eyebrow.

"Uh, yeah. Where were you during the zombie turkey plague last Thanksgiving?"

"I took the weekend off and went up to my folks in Roxbury."

"Massachusetts? Were you affected by the plague that hit the turkey farms in western Massachusetts?"

"No, but I read about them in the paper. And I saw the videos online."

"Do you have a feel for what a zombie human might be like?"

"Nothing I want to tangle with."

"That's all I have."

They left, and Boxer said, "The last girl is Vida Loca. Apartment 3C."

"What about 3D?" Sam asked as they walked around the corner.

"Empty. They're trying to rent it now."

After Boxer knocked on the door, a tall woman with long, straight black hair, deep tan, black eyes, and a striking figure opened the door. Sam thought she looked like the oldest call girl they'd met, perhaps thirty.

"Police? I'm glad you're here. When can I get into Layla's apartment?"

"You're Vida Loca, right?"

"That's me."

"When you can get into her apartment is up to the forensics team, whenever they're done with it. I'll call them after we're done. But first we'd like to ask you some questions."

"About Layla's murder? Of course." She spoke confidently and gestured them inside.

Vida seated them around a coffee table with a white leather couch and matching chairs.

"When did you first meet Layla?" Poodles asked.

"About nine months ago. I was working Park Avenue, and she asked if I'd like to go into business with her. I agreed provisionally, as long as my income stream stayed the same or picked up."

"So how did that work out for you?" Poodles asked matter of factly.

"Great. I got more clients, and they paid more, even with Layla's cut."

"What was Layla's cut? Fifty percent?"

"No, that's what pimps charge. She charged ten percent plus expenses, so it came to about twenty percent."

"What expenses?"

"The apartment, utilities, any legal fees, medical benefits, insurance, that kind of stuff."

"Taxes?" Sam asked.

"Yes. We're registered as an LLC, Park Avenue Escort Services. We've got the highest ratings on Yelp."

"Were you here two nights ago, on the eleventh?" Poodles asked.

"Yes. I work every night I can."

"What did you see and hear?"

"Nothing but my client. These rooms are pretty well insulated."

"No yelling, no police?"

"No. I was occupied with my client until the next morning, when he left."

"When did you find out about the murder?" Boxer asked, his eyes full of sympathy.

"I slept until one o'clock like I usually do. I went out for a walk and a nosh, and I saw all the police tape. I knocked on Bethany's and Shawna's doors, but they weren't there. I checked my phone as I ate pastrami and rye, and found out about the murder."

"What a way to find out. Did you tell anyone about it?"

"No. I was mostly worried about the money in her safe and the business records. Layla tracks—or tracked—the business on a spreadsheet on her computer. I had a client last night too, so I had to get ready for him, and I wanted to make sure all the income and expenses were still tracked."

"Did Layla show you the spreadsheet?"

"Yes. She was training me how to run it. I'd get more money, and she'd get more time."

"So you're thinking of running the escort service yourself?"

"Someone has to do it. Bethany doesn't want to, and Shawna isn't interested in business."

"Do you know why someone would want Layla murdered?" Boxer took over the interview.

Vida pressed her full lips together and furrowed her brow. "I don't think Layla had any enemies. But you never know."

"Have you seen this man before?" Boxer showed her the picture of the zombie.

"He wasn't one of my clients. He might have been one of Layla's."

"You haven't seen him before, anywhere?"

"I don't think so. I see so many men, both mine and those going to the other girls, I can't remember them all."

"Do you know anyone else who can shed light on this?"

"Check with the night maintenance man. He might have heard or seen someone. He's on the first floor."

"Is there anything else you want to tell me that I haven't asked you?"

Vida put her finger to her pursed lips. "Layla always seemed very eager to make more money, more clients, higher rates. I wonder if she ticked off one of her customers? This zombie might have been one of them."

"Does she have a list of her customers?" Poodles leaned in toward Vida, looming over her.

"If she does, I've never seen it. It'd be like her to have a list though."

Boxer looked at Poodles. "We can check with forensics. I think they have her laptop."

"Thank you, Vida," Poodles said. "Sam, do you have anything?"

"Yeah. Vida, do you think Layla would take a zombie guy as her customer?"

"Sure, if she didn't know about it. He might have become a zombie after he became her client. But as long as he paid, she wouldn't care. We're open minded, diverse, and nondiscriminatory here."

"I guess that's all." Sam started to turn away and then turned back, "Oh, Vida, where did you get your interest in business?"

"I guess I always liked numbers. My dad owned a dry cleaner, and I helped him with the books. An escort service is a lot like a dry cleaner."

"OK. I would never have thought of that."

"You come in for a service, and that service is scheduled and delivered, and then you pay for your goods. It's exactly the same."

"Thanks, Vida." Sam left with Boxer and Poodles.

* * *

On the way back to the station, Poodles looked at Sam in the backseat. "So how do you recommend catching this zombie?"

Sam stopped gawking at the skyscrapers. "We set a trap for him."

"Where?"

"First place will be the apartment block. Put steel netting around the third floor and the windows."

"How do we even know he'll come there?"

"Oh. I assumed he'd come back. The other thing I thought of was tracking the girls and seeing if any of them have seen the zombie or if he meets them. Say, what about the building security cameras? What did they show about that night? Did they show him entering the building?"

"We'll find out right now." Boxer parked the car. "We'll go to forensics and see what they've found before we do anything."

At the forensics lab, a slim brunette named Mary O'Kelly met them. "Hello, Boxer, Poodles." She looked at Sam.

"This is Sam Melvin, private eye," Boxer said. "What have you found out about the Langoria case?"

"Not much from the blood samples. It's all Layla's. Nothing from the assailant."

"No surprise there," Sam murmured.

Mary looked sharply at Sam. "Oh? Why wouldn't a violent assailant leave some blood behind?"

"Because he's a zombie. His skin is tougher and heals faster than a normal human."

"I'd heard that, but I didn't realize the implications."

"What about the building security video?" Boxer asked.

"We've got a good image of him entering the building and the elevator."

"What about the third floor?" Poodles said.

"That camera was out, unfortunately."

"Is it fixed now?" Sam asked.

"I don't know. That's the building's responsibility."

"I'll check with them. We need to keep an eye on that building."

"We'll go with you, Sam. We need to interview the superintendent too," Boxer said.

"What did the ME find out from the autopsy?" Poodles looked down at the much shorter technician.

"Avulsed neck. Cranial amputation. Massive loss of blood."

"Cause of death?"

"Decapitation."

"Nothing else?"

"What else would you expect?"

"Any drugs in her system?"

"No."

"Any other marks on her?"

"Nothing but vaccination scars."

"What are you looking for, Poodles?" Sam asked,

"I'm looking for any other lead. I'm suspicious of this whole situation. It seems too obvious."

"You're always suspicious, Poodles." Boxer smiled broadly. "That's what I like about you."

"I'm glad I meet with your approval."

"Sarcasm noted."

Poodles smirked. That was the first time Sam had seen her smile.

"What's so obvious?" Sam asked.

"The murder suspect, the zombie guy. Everyone is cooperating. That's just not normal."

As they walked out, Boxer said, "We've got two problems. Find the murdering zombie. And catch him."

"Three problems. We also need to stay alive." Poodles looked back at Boxer as she strode to the car and scooted onto the driver's seat.

Sam filed into the back, as usual. *I'll be happy if those are the only problems.* He felt uneasy about the whole case.

Boxer's phone rang. "Boxer here. . . . Oh, where? . . . When? . . . This morning at eight. We'll be right there." He tapped End. "Poodles, head for East Ninety-Eighth and step on it." Boxer turned on the siren and the flashing light in the back window.

Poodles, without batting an eye, skidded the car around on Park Avenue and headed toward Ninety-Eighth.

"What's up?" Poodles asked as she drove at seventy down Park Avenue.

"Another madam's been beheaded."

Chapter 13 – To Catch a Zombie

As Poodles drove them to the murder location—an alley off Park Avenue—Boxer read off the information he had on the victim from his laptop.

"Madelaine 'Madam' Maxime was born in New Jersey as Jane Seymour in 1964. Thirty-eight arrests on vice charges, mostly in the eighties and nineties. None since 2010. She was running Park Avenue Escort Service at the time of death. Death by decapitation. Head not found. Forensics now on the scene."

Sam swallowed back nausea.

"Here we are." Poodles kept the flasher on and double-parked next to the alley.

They met a slim, dark-haired man in a lab coat on the sidewalk.

"Hi, Boxer, Poodles."

"Hi, Harry. Sam, this is Harry Fairchild, head of forensics What've ya found out so far?" Boxer said.

"Madam Maxime was killed in this alley no more than an hour ago. We've collected our samples, taken our pictures, and they're on the way to the lab. If you want to take a look around, you'll be the first after us."

Poodles stepped over the police tape. Sam, Boxer, and Harry followed her. She stopped short.

"You get that footprint, Harry?" She pointed at a heel imprint in the dirt.

"You bet, Poodles. There are a few more. Can you find them all?"

They scanned the ground. "There's a high-heel mark." Poodles pointed to the side of the alley.

Harry nodded. "It matches with the shoes Maxime was wearing at the time of death."

"There's a smudge. It looks like a shoe," Sam said.

"That matches the heel print. Man's size ten."

"And there's another of the left foot in the blood smear over there," Boxer said.

"You got them all."

"Do you have any witnesses?" Poodles asked.

"None. We got an anonymous call on the tip line at eight this morning and found her body about eight twenty. No one reported hearing or seeing anything this morning or last night. The body was still warm when we got here."

The three scanned the alley. Aside from the footsteps and the big blood spot, with the outline where the body was found, there was nothing else.

"Where does the alley end?" Sam asked.

"Madison Avenue," Boxer said.

"Just like Monopoly. Let's walk down and see if we see anything."

They came to the end of the alley, and it was blocked by a ten-foot cast-iron fence. Boxer looked at the spikes. "I don't think anyone came in or out this way."

Sam shook his head. "Nah. That's no problem for a zombie to go over."

"Regardless, Sam, there are no more clues here. Let's figure out how to catch this guy." Poodles turned back.

"First, we've got to be where he is and where he'll be next," Boxer said.

"Before that let's see if he showed up at the scene of the first crime."

"What's before first?" Poodles stared at Sam.

"Zeroeth?"

She grimaced.

At least I got a half smile out of her.

"This guy's getting away with murder. We've got to do whatever it takes to stop him."

"The superintendent promised to fix the security cameras. Let's see if they got anything." They trooped to the car. Sam rode in the back while Poodles maneuvered through Manhattan traffic to the Elysian apartment complex.

They went en masse to the security office and asked to see the video recordings of the previous night.

"Front-door recordings first," Boxer said.

Watching the replay at high speed, Poodles shouted, "Stop! I think that's the zombie guy."

They replayed the segment from midnight to twelve thirty. At 12:12, a guy entered in a heavy coat, scarf, and hood. He didn't remove anything but went right to the elevator.

"Maybe. We'll have to look at the third-floor recording to be sure," Boxer said.

"Notice that he had a key? Maybe he lives here."

"Could be, Sam. Or he just made a copy."

"Isn't that illegal?"

"So is murder, Sam." Poodles stared at him.

"Let's try the third-floor camera now," Sam said.

The security guard played it. The camera blacked out at 8:00 p.m. and didn't go back on.

"Crap. Sorry, guys. Something blipped out. I'll go check it at shift change."

"We'll check it now." Poodles left, and they followed her.

"It might be useless, but let's dust the elevator buttons for fingerprints." Boxer pulled out his kit and dusted the whole panel, pulling off dozens of them.

He was still working on that when they reached the third floor. "We'll check the camera." Poodles and Sam walked down the hall to the camera.

"That's simple but effective." Poodles pointed to the camera in the upper corner of the hall. Black tape covered its lens. She jumped up and pulled off the tape.

"You could play basketball."

"I did."

"Simple and effective, but not effective enough." Sam moved to the corner.

"What do you mean, Sam?"

"Look here." Sam reached down into the potted plant in the corner and pulled out another camera. "I put this here when I nagged the superintendent to fix the camera. I wanted a backup."

"That's good thinking. Let's see what it caught."

Sam played back the last twelve hours, displaying it on his tablet.

"I'm glad you got a fisheye lens," Poodles said. "We can see both halls from here. There are the call girls. And their customers. And they leave. We're coming up to midnight. Slow it down, Sam. There he is!"

Sam could see the zombie guy come up from the stairway, go down the hall, and stride around the corner. He had the same coat on, but the hat, scarf, and gloves were off.

"That's the way to Vida's apartment. Did you put a camera in the other corner?"

"No. I didn't think of it."

Boxer had joined them and watched the end of the replay. "What do you think, Poodles? Should we confront Vida?"

"We don't know for sure he went into her room. We just know he passed Bethany's and Shawna's rooms. I'd like to place another camera in the other corner. I don't want there to be any possibility of denial."

"OK, but let's also get the steel net ready."

"I'm liking how you think, Sam. How big are they?"

"The ones used by the Chicago police were about the size of a suitcase. They used compressed air to shoot out the net."

"Won't that be obvious?"

"Not if we hide it. They used big plant pots in Chicago. I think we can put one in front of Vida's door. What kind of plants should we use?"

"Philodendrons or fichus would blend in. They're used for indoor decoration."

"All right, Poodles. You get the plants. Sam, you get the net. Can you borrow one from the Chicago police department?"

"Sure. Superintendent Howell likes me. If not, I can get Chief Dirkse to help."

"Sam, even I like you."

"Poodles. I didn't know you cared."

"Don't let it go to your head. You're barely above average."

"That's the story of my life."

* * *

The steel net box arrived the next day at the NYPD police headquarters. Boxer and Poodles placed security cameras around the other known escort services in the area and added a camera covering the other two halls of the third floor of the Elysian apartments.

"Where'd you hide it, Poodles?"

"In between the philodendron and the fichus tree, on top of the net box. I put in a microphone as well."

"We've got all the cameras on the police secure wireless and can monitor them from our office." Boxer showed Sam the new monitors with dozens of camera feeds mounted on the walls of their office.

"I also got six unknown prints off the elevator and three off the stair railing. One on the railing matched one on the elevator."

"Did you get any off Layla's door?"

"No. That's a good idea, Sam."

"I can hardly wait for tonight. Let's see if we catch this guy."

"Cool your jets. We've got eight hours to midnight, if he returns at the same time he did last night."

"OK. I'll review what these cameras caught. We've got twelve feeds plus the two on the third floor?"

"Yeah. Go ahead and knock yourself out. Poodles and I are going to the deli."

"Oh. I guess this can wait. I'll join you."

* * *

As midnight neared, even Poodles and Boxer hovered around the monitors. Sam listed all the food deliveries on the third floor that evening. Nothing had happened for two hours.

"Maybe he won't show." Boxer glanced at the clock. Twelve twenty-three.

"That'd be our usual luck." Poodles looked glummer than usual.

"Hey." Sam pointed. A man came out of the stairwell, looked up and down the hall, and went to Vida's door.

"That's him." Poodles sounded satisfied.

"Fire the net?" Sam looked at Boxer.

"No. Get him on the way out, when he's relaxed and unprepared."

"That may not be until tomorrow morning."

"It's already tomorrow morning, Poodles."

"I mean daybreak."

"Or even into the afternoon."

"Don't these guys have a real life? Doesn't this zombie have to work for a living?"

"Now that's a good question, Sam. I hope we get to ask him."

Three hours later, Sam awoke from his chair when Poodles said, "There he is."

Wide awake now, Sam watched the zombie close the door and turn. Boxer pushed a button on his screen.

BAM! The net exploded out from under the camera and partially enveloped the man. He turned and pounded on the door. The side toward the door was partially open. He hauled the net up from his knees, tossed it over his head, and shook it off. The door opened, and he reentered Vida's apartment. They heard pounding feet, then tinkling glass. Vida leaned on the door, looking shaken. She pulled out her phone from the back pocket of her jeans and dialed a number. Boxer's phone rang.

"Boxer, what the hell did you do? I had an explosion outside my door, and a net almost caught my last customer."

"That was the zombie we're trying to catch. What's his name?"

"Fred. Fred Flintstone."

"C'mon, be straight with me."

"A lot of customers give us phony names. That was his. We take cash from anyone, even cavemen."

"Or zombies." Poodle grimaced.

"Is that you, Poodles?"

"Yeah." Boxer handed her the phone and took out another one.

"Is Sam there too?"

"Yeah."

"I might as well be on the internet for all the privacy I've got."

"If you want privacy, you're in the wrong business."

"Or you've got the wrong customers," Sam said.

Boxer put down his other phone and took the first one back. "Hey, Vida. Just stay where you are and don't touch anything. We'll be there in a few minutes, and so will forensics."

"I'll sit next to these nice plants. Did you guys put them here?"

"Yeah."

"I thought the building management was just upping the décor to charge us more rent."

"See you soon, Vida." Boxer hung up.

* * *

"OK Vida, why did you take a zombie as a customer?" Boxer confronted Vida in her room. They'd covered up the broken window after the forensics team had taken fingerprints. The room was still chilly.

"How would I know he was a zombie? He had dark-brown eyes."

"Boxer, zombies can wear colored contact lenses." Sam rubbed a hand behind his neck.

"Now you tell us, Sam." Boxer sounded as exasperated as he ever had. "He could be anywhere in the city. How will we find him? Tell me, zombie man." He glared at Sam.

"He probably works a regular job. He seems to like Vida, so maybe he'll come back here."

"He'd be an idiot to come back."

"Criminals tend to return to the scene of the crime."

"How long have you been a detective?"

"Almost a month."

"Twenty years for me. How about you Poodles?"

"Ten years."

Boxer took a deep breath. "OK, Sam. You focus on the apartment building. We'll follow other leads. Let's go, Poodles."

* * *

Sam spent the day reviewing the camera feeds. Vida went to sleep and didn't stir until 3:00 p.m. The other girls came and went as usual. Several packages were delivered from the biggest mail-order firm. Chinese food arrived for Bethany, pizza for Shawna. A butcher delivered a large package of meat, neatly wrapped in white paper. *Huh. I didn't know butchers delivered. Maybe in New York City.*

Toward the evening, hamburgers arrived at Vida's apartment. Then about ten o'clock, a deep-dish meat-lovers pizza arrived. Hmmm. *That's a lot of food. Even for two.*

Unable to figure it out, Sam went back to his hotel and bed.

* * *

The next morning Sam, Boxer, and Poodles discussed their findings.

"I interviewed seven madams in the area, and Poodles interviewed five. Here's what I found out." Boxer held up a notebook. "None of them have seen our suspect at any time. Most of them have had cordial relations with Layla and Maxime. Some thought Layla was getting uppity by becoming a madam, but none seemed to have a motive to kill her or know anyone who did. That's it." Boxer frowned and looked at Poodles.

"I found two who thought they might have seen the guy, but they weren't sure. None of them cared about Layla. None of them had, or could think of, a motive to kill her."

"That's it? That took you twelve hours?" Sam shook his head in puzzlement.

"More like fourteen," Boxer said.

"What did *you* do? Better, what did you *accomplish?*" Poodles looked daggers at Sam.

"Um. I found that Vida is eating a lot. She even ordered a pair of subs this morning."

Boxer snorted. Poodles looked even angrier.

"No clues? No leads? Why is Detective Howell even paying you?"

"Uh, I thought that was a clue. Maybe Vida is hiding the zombie in her apartment. Zombies have a high metabolism and eat a lot."

"I was wrong. I thought the idea of zombie going back to the apartment building was the stupidest idea I'd ever heard. Now I think this idea is." Boxer looked disgusted.

"Exactly. That's why it's a great idea. No one would expect it or look for it. Suppose the two are in cahoots. Or in love. 'The things you do for love,'" Sam sang.

Boxer rolled his eyes. Poodles looked puzzled.

"Anyway, I want to set up the net trap outside the apartment window. Then, let's get a search warrant to look for the zombie."

"Farfetched. I wouldn't give you a warrant for that," Boxer said.

"Hmmm. It's a long shot, but it might work. Even if the zombie isn't there, we might find evidence of him in Vida's apartment," Poodles said.

"Wait. You're supposed to be the skeptical one, Poodles."

"Sometimes Boxer and I switch roles. It really confuses suspects."

"Am I a suspect?"

"Nah. You're too harmless and naïve," Boxer said.

"Thanks, I guess. So how do we get a warrant?"

"Just present your idea to the DA and hope. I wonder how you'll get the net mounted without anyone seeing it?" Boxer still looked skeptical.

"I got an idea," Sam said

"Let's go to the DA first." Poodles jingled her car keys.

* * *

"I honestly didn't think you'd get the search warrant."

"You guys backed me up. Thanks, Boxer, Poodles."

"We argue a lot between ourselves, but we're on your side ultimately. We want to get this guy," Poodles said.

"Sometimes it's the wacky ideas that work. Now, Sam, what's your idea about catching the zombie outside the window? It's a sheer drop to the back alley."

"First, let's stop here." Sam pointed at a pawn shop.

"A pawn shop? Why?" Poodles double-parked and turned on the flasher.

"You'll see." Sam ran into the shop. He came out a few minutes later, struggling under the burden of a huge window air conditioner. He pushed it into the backseat and then sat next to it.

"So you plan to hide the net with the air conditioner?" Poodles looked around at him and the air conditioner and then drove toward the apartment building.

"Basically."

"How will you install it in Vida's apartment without her suspecting something?"

"I won't. We'll put it in the apartment above hers."

"I like it. Even if it doesn't work, that's a good idea."

"Thanks, Boxer."

"I'm driving there now," Poodles interjected.

Boxer helped Sam carry the air conditioner into the elevator. They went to the fourth floor and apartment 4C. Meanwhile, Poodles went to 3C and retrieved the net trap from under the plants.

"How will we approach this?" Boxer asked.

"Let me handle this. I've got an idea."

A middle-aged lady answered the door. Chains rattled as she peeked through the door gap at Sam.

"What do you want?" She frowned at him.

"Hi, ma'am. I've got a free air conditioner for you to try out. If you like it, you get to keep it. We just want your recommendation for our company."

"Sounds suspicious. Let me see it."

Boxer pushed the air conditioner forward into her view.

"That's looks used. Why would you give me an old air conditioner?"

"That's our business model. We buy old air conditioners and refurbish them and then sell or rent them out at low prices."

"Huh. I've never heard of that before. What's the name of your company?"

"Sam's. Sam's Super Cool AC."

"And you're Sam?"

"You bet."

"You look harmless enough. And goodness knows, it's hot in here in the summer. C'mon in."

Boxer helped Sam hang it out the window. Then Poodles came in with the box holding the net trap.

"What's that?"

"That's our custom add-on that makes the AC super effective." Sam smiled at her.

"OK. Get it added on. Say, why are you doing this in the winter?"

"It's our off season. We're too busy working in the summer to do this promotion stuff."

"Oh."

They needed Poodles's long arms and legs to "install" the add-on from the adjacent window. She pointed the box downward and strapped it around the air conditioner.

"Now test it. I want to make sure this isn't some scam."

"Sure, ma'am." Sam plugged it in and turned it on. A frigid blast sputtered out.

"Whoa! Turn it off. That's super effective all right. That should help in the summer. I get to keep this, right?"

"You bet. Thanks for your time, ma'am. Don't forget—Sam's Super Cool AC."

"I won't. Thanks, Sam."

"Bye."

After they closed the door, Poodles giggled. Boxer looked at her, stunned.

"What's tickling your funny bone?" Sam asked.

"You. That line of BS you fed her was hilarious. I couldn't keep a straight face."

"That's the first time I've ever heard you giggle in ten years. Anyway, this is your baby, Sam. When do you want the arrest warrant served? Now?"

"Why not? We're here. We're ready. I'll monitor the camera on the net trap and fire it if the guy goes out the window."

"We'll serve the warrant to Vida and make sure no one is inside but her."

"Thanks, Poodles."

Sam stayed by the plants, watching the camera feed on his tablet, as Boxer and Poodles knocked on Vida's door.

The door opened. "Oh, it's you. What do you want? You woke me up." She sounded sleepy.

"We'd like to search your apartment."

"For what? I don't have any drugs or anything."

"We suspect a person of interest is hiding here."

"What? I don't have anyone in here. You'll have to get a search warrant anyway."

"Here it is. Please open the door." Boxer was at his most genial.

"No."

"You can't say no to a search warrant—you *have* to open the door." Poodles put her foot in the door so Vida couldn't close it.

"You're invading my privacy! You have no right! There's no one here but me!" Her voice rose louder and louder even as she backed away from the door.

"Help me with this door chain, Boxer." Together they pushed the door and broke the chain.

"This'll just take a few minutes, Vida." They came in with their guns out and ready. Vida ran into the bedroom.

"Follow her." Poodles stalked forward, and Boxer backed her up. Sam peered around the two.

When they reached the door, a man rolled out from under the bed—bearded, swarthy, with black eyes.

"That's him!" Poodles pointed her fléchette rifle at him. "Don't move, mister. You're under—"

The zombie leapt to the door, smashed the gun from her hand, and pushed past her.

Boxer shot him in the back as he zoomed toward the window. Vida screamed.

The zombie dove through the window.

POOM! The net blew down and enveloped him like a manta ray.

"Got him!" Sam yelled from the hall. "Come and help me!"

Sam ran into the stairwell and down the steps, two and three at a time, while keeping on ear on the conversation behind him.

"I didn't think he could move that fast," Poodles noted, her feet pounding down the stairs.

"He's surprised me more than once." At Boxer's voice, Same spun for a quick peek to see Boxer sliding down the railing, hitting each landing with two feet and bouncing to the next railing.

Sam continued his sprint out the fire door and saw the zombie violently struggling against the steel netting. He darted to the left.

"Where's Sam?" he heard Poodles ask.

"Look at him! He's going to get out if we—"

"Here I am!" Sam ran into the alley carrying a shotgun. "I had to get this to stop him." He pointed the shotgun at the zombie.

"You have the right to remain silent—" Boxer began.

BLAM! The zombie, peppered by rock salt, slumped to the ground.

"Sam, you're supposed to read them him his rights first," Poodles reproved.

"With zombies, you don't have time. With human zombies, it's blam or be slammed." Sam pumped the shotgun. "I'd better give him another dose."

"Wait—"

BLAM! The zombie, bleeding from hundreds of spots, recoiled from the blast and lay on the ground.

"This isn't legal, Sam."

"Right, but we don't have time. It took two shotgun blasts and a twenty-story fall to get the other zombie out of commission. This one only had a three-story fall and a little net. He was close to escaping."

Poodles snapped handcuffs on the guy. "Do you mind sharing the backseat with this guy, Sam?"

"No. Do you mind if I blast him again if he starts moving?"

"Would it make any difference if I did?"

"Uh, no."

Poodles rolled her eyes and climbed into the car. Sam and Boxer heaved the limp body into the backseat.

"I gotta say, Sam, your idea worked."

"I'm glad it did, Boxer. It was a little touch and go until I got the shotgun from the car."

"Is he stirring at all? I can't believe he's not dead, even from just rock salt. Those blasts were *close.*"

"Ha. Listen, Poodles—most of his cuts and wounds have already closed from the zombie bacteria. The salt's slowly dissolving, killing the bacteria. The biggest wound's gone from a dinner plate to a silver-dollar size. If it weren't for the salt, he'd be up and at me."

"I guess this isn't your first time around the zombie block."

"No, it isn't."

* * *

"Hey, Lisa! Guess what? I caught the zombie!" Sam was so eager to share his success that he called her from the police station as they turned the zombie over to the jail officers. Despite two shots of rock salt, he wasn't cured of his zombiism. They kept him in handcuffs and leg irons as he was processed.

"That's great! Uh, who's that in the background?" Lisa peered from his tablet and craned her neck to look over Sam's shoulder.

Sam glanced behind him. "Oh, that's Poodles. She's one of the detectives I work with."

"She's awfully good looking. Too good looking. Have you been cheating on me?" Lisa was furious.

"Uh, no Lisa. Never crossed my mind."

"Well, it crossed my mind a lot, as you've been hanging with all these hookers a thousand miles away from me."

"Put your mind at ease, Lisa. You're the only one for me."

"I'll just make sure. I'll see you tonight in New York."

"What? Are you sure? What about the paper?"

"I can run it remotely. Most of our revenue comes from our videos anyway. Bye, and don't do anything I'd kill you for."

"Wait—" The tablet went blank.

"Problems, Sam?" Boxer asked him kindly.

"Uh, no, it's just my wife."

"Is she the jealous sort?"

"I didn't think so, but now she's coming here to check on me. She's jealous over Poodles!"

"I can see that. How long have you been married?"

"Coming up on our three-month anniversary in a week or so."

"So you don't know her at all."

"Whatdaya mean? I've known her since high school, fifteen years."

"But that's just on the surface. You don't know the inside until you've been married for at least a year. Take it from me. I know."

"Have you been married a long time?"

"Twenty years, but it seems longer. I'm on my fifth wife."

"Oh. Sorry to hear that, I guess."

"Nah, she's great. The best one yet. Not at all jealous."

"What are you guys talking about? I overheard a little, and it sounded like you were giving Sam marital advice," Poodles said.

"I was. He's having a bout of a jealous wife."

"Lisa's coming here to make sure I don't cheat on her."

"What set her off? Did she see you with someone?" Poodles asked.

"Yeah. You."

"Me?" Poodles looked surprised.

"Yeah. She said don't do anything she'd have to kill me over."

"You're not even my type, Sam."

"I kind of knew that. But you'll have a chance to explain to her. She'll be here tonight."

"This is all very entertaining, but we've got a zombie murderer to interview. Let's go." Boxer led them to the jail cells.

The police had taken out the zombie's contact lenses while he was unconscious, and his eyes glowed in the cell. He looked at Sam. "Melvin! I'll get you!" He threw himself at the cage bars, gritting his teeth and trying to bend them. They creaked alarmingly but held.

He sat down on the floor of the cell, his shoulders sagging in despair.

"We just have a few questions for you," Boxer began.

No answer.

"We're here get a few facts. They might help you get out of jail. What's your name?" Boxer turned on his charm, beaming at him like he was his best friend.

He turned his glowing red eyes to Boxer. "Does it really matter?"

"What should we call you?"

"Sebastian."

"How'd you know my name, Sebastian?" Sam couldn't hold back his question.

"It's all over the news. You're the big zombie expert helping the police. Thanks for nothing."

"So, Sebastian, what kind of work do you do?"

"I'm a pest control guy at Pest-B-Gone."

"Work regular eight-hour days?"

"Yeah, when it's not twelve or fifteen. We guarantee to get rid of all pests in a day."

"That's quite a promise."

"That's why we're so busy and growing so fast." He sounded proud.

"How long you've been there?"

"Five years. I'm one of their senior guys."

"So what happened that night, last Tuesday the eleventh?"

"Oh that." He sighed. "I came by to see Vida. She's my favorite, you know. I saw the door to 3F was open, and I peeked in. There was this gal on the floor. I checked her, and she was dead as a doornail."

"Where'd you find her?"

"Behind the couch."

"Then what happened?"

"I didn't want to get involved, so I left her and went on to Vida's apartment."

"Did you spend the night?"

"Of course. You would too."

"So when did you go into Ms. Longoria's apartment?"

"A little before twelve."

"And when did you leave?"

"A little afterward. I didn't want to stick around."

"Did you see anyone else?"

"Nope, just Vida, afterward."

"Did you know Ms. Longoria?"

"Just to see her. I knew she ran this escort service, and I think she knew I was seeing Vida."

"No other connections?"

"Nope."

"Do you have any evidence you were there and that she was already dead? How could you tell?"

"I checked her pulse. There was none. She wasn't breathing. That's dead to me."

"Were there any marks on her body?"

"Nope." Boxer looked at Poodles, and she motioned he should continue.

"Is there anyone else we should talk to who knew about the incident or the circumstances surrounding it?"

"I can't think of anyone."

"Have you talked to anyone about the incident? Who? What did you tell them?"

"Well yeah. I told Vida about it."

"When?"

"Around noon—no, make it one, after we woke and had brunch."

Boxer stopped and looked at Poodles.

"There seems to be a problem here, Mr.—" Poodles looked inquiringly at him.

"Filmore. My full name's Sebastian Filmore. What's the problem?"

"We have you on security camera ripping the head off Ms. Longoria."

"You do? Well crap. You found out."

"So why did you kill her?"

"Oh, I didn't. She was still dead when I found her."

"What? Why in the world would you rip her head off?"

"Because I like heads. Mwah-ha-ha-hah! I have a whole collection of them!" He stood up, laughing like a maniac. "Birds, dogs, cats—and now people!" He came close to the bars, close to Poodles. Spittle dripped down his chin.

"I didn't kill her," he whispered. "But maybe I'll kill you. And you." He looked at Boxer. "And especially you!" His eyes pierced Sam's like laser beams. "Mwah-ha-ha!" He danced and capered around the cell while laughing loudly.

"Mr. Filmore! We've got more questions for you!"

"Mwah-ha-ha! It's much easier to dance when you're a zombie. You never get tired!" He danced on.

"Mr. Filmore! This is life or death for you." Boxer tried to interrupt him.

"Life? Death? What's the difference when you're a zombie? Mwah-ha-ha! This is the dance of life and death!" He doubled his speed, bouncing from wall to wall, shaking the bars as he kicked off them. He never stopped laughing.

Sam motioned that they should leave the crazed the crazed zombie. Sam could hear the zombie's laughter all the way back to the elevator.

"Well, that was a failure," Boxer said after the doors closed.

"Maybe I shouldn't have confronted him about the video we had," Poodles said. "Maybe I shouldn't have butted into your interrogation."

"No, it doesn't matter. I think he had this planned out."

"What?" Sam and Poodles said together.

"I think he's pulling an insanity act to get away with murder."

"He can't get away with that!" Sam said indignantly.

"Many have, Sam. Many have."

* * *

There was a knock on Sam's hotel door at ten o'clock that evening.

"Who is it?"

"Lisa. Lemme in!" She pounded on the door.

"Course. Hi, hon—oof!" Lisa tackled him to the floor and kicked the door closed.

"What's going on?" Sam looked up at her.

"You're going to convince me you've not cheated on me."

* * *

"Sebastian Filmore has been arraigned for murder," Boxer said the next day in their office. Then he looked at Sam. "What's up with you, Sam? You look like you haven't slept."

"I didn't."

"What happened?" Poodles asked.

"Lisa showed up last night."

Boxer chuckled. "I take it you made up."

"Yeah, enough that Lisa's gone out shopping on Fifth Avenue. She was whistling."

Both of them laughed. "I guess we won't need you anymore, except to testify at the trial."

"OK. I'd still like to talk with Sebastian."

"After that whole crazy act?"

"Yeah. Maybe he'll slip up."

* * *

"Did he?" Boxer asked the next morning.

"Did he what?" Sam was confused.

"Did he slip up?"

"Not really. He still maintains his story. I went through all the questions you asked, and now he says he left through the window, just as we saw on the video. He didn't see Vida again until the night before we caught him."

"That's interesting. I've got something for you."

"What's that?"

"His girlfriend Vida saw him in prison too. Here's the video and audio recording."

Boxer played the recording on his tablet. Vida came into the cell room and sat on a folding chair in front of the bars. Sebastian rose from bed and stood in front of her.

"Hi, Vida."

"Hi, Sebastian."

"Sorry I got caught."

"Don't worry. I'll get you out somehow."

"The trial's in two days."

"Yeah. I know."

"Think I'll get off?"

"Maybe."

"I've got a public defender. I saw him today.

"So what does he think?"

"He talks a good game, like he'll create sufficient doubt since I lack a motive. But the video's a killer."

"I know. Maybe they'll make a mistake."

"Maybe."

"Time's up." The jailer came in.

"Here's a note for you. I love you."

"No notes. Give it back." She leveled a shotgun at him.

Sebastian glanced at the note, smiled, and swallowed it. "Try to get it." He grinned at the shotgun.

"No more visits for you." The jailer hauled Vida out of the room, while Sebastian laughed.

Sam looked up from the screen. "I wonder what she wrote."

"Why don't you ask him, Sam?" Poodles suggested.

"I'll do that, right now."

* * *

"Hi, Sebastian."

"I wondered if you'd come back."

"I heard your girlfriend, Vida, came by."

"Yeah. That was nice of her."

"Tomorrow's the trial. Do you think they'll believe you?"

"I don't know. Do you believe me?"

"I'm not sure. If you're not the murderer, then who is? You've got to come up with the real murderer."

"That's a problem, but not my problem. That's your problem. You're the great detective."

"Me? No, I'm just a reporter pretending to be a detective. I just know a lot about zombies."

"Will an electric chair kill a zombie? Say a zombie human, for instance."

"I don't know." Sam paused. "Maybe not. It'd have to kill all the zombie bacteria."

"Wow. What does it take to kill a zombie then?"

"zombie turkeys have to be split into at least two pieces. I don't know about zombie people. The zombiism seems different."

"How?"

"It seems the bacteria are more resilient in people. With turkeys, a saltwater spray cured them. With people, it takes an injection."

"So why didn't the rock salt do it?"

"Not enough of it, I guess. It took about forty shots for a bull. It took a shot in the face to get the guy in Chicago. And he fell twenty stories too."

"Huh. I guess I'm a living experiment."

"Yeah. Say, if it's not too personal, what did Vida write you on the note?"

A big smile covered his face. "I didn't tell the other guys, but you're a regular guy. It was short and sweet. 'I love you.'"

"That's sweet."

"Time's up." The jailer came in, and Sam left.

* * *

"Wow, Lisa! You look like a million bucks!" Sam stopped and stared as he met Lisa in the lobby of One Police Plaza.

"Ha! It didn't cost that much, but almost." She twirled in her new skirt and blouse of muted beige.

"You look like one of those starlets from the forties."

"That's the effect I was going for, complete with the hairstyling."

"Oh yeah. Now that you mention it, I see you've changed it."

"And my makeup."

"Oh, are you wearing any?"

"You doofus. You're such a guy." Her brows furrowed into her normal scowl. "Is that Poodles?"

Sam turned and saw Poodles running toward them.

"Yes. I wonder what's wrong."

"Sam! Oh, hi, you must be Lisa."

"And you are Poodles." Lisa glared at her.

"No time for jealousy. Sebastian's been killed."

"What? How?" Sam cried.

"What a great story!" Lisa pulled out a tablet that matched her Coach purse. She dropped her purse onto the floor and sat on it while she typed.

"How? He was blown up. Someone smuggled in a bomb."

179

Chapter 14 – The Last Victim

Sam, Lisa, Poodles, and Boxer watched the video from the cell. Over and over.

His meal was delivered. He ate. He lay down to sleep. Something rolled from under his bed toward the cell door. A blinding flash and explosion shook the camera and bent the cell bars.

Sam couldn't quite figure it out.

The blast flipped the bed and smashed Sebastian against the wall. For a second he stuck there, flattened unnaturally. Then his leg fell off. His arm and his head followed. Then the other arm. Finally, his body slid down the wall, leaving a smear of blood. When the leg hit the floor, it rolled away.

"That was one thorough explosion," Lisa said.

"You're not grossed out?" Poodles asked.

"Nah. I'm nothing like Sam."

"Opposites attract," Boxer said.

"That's for sure. We're as opposite as you can get." Poodles snickered.

"Maybe I'll like you. Sam and I are total opposites too." Lisa sent Sam a loving glance.

"I don't need people to like me. I'm not a people person."

"Neither am I." That made Lisa shift her look back to Poodles.

"This girl talk is wonderful, but let's consider who'd want to kill Sebastian," Boxer said.

"His enemies," Sam said.

"Layla's friends," Lisa said.

"Or Maxime's friends," Poodles added.

"Or someone else we're not thinking of," Boxer finished.

"That should be a finite list. You've got Layla's spreadsheet." Lisa pointed to a laptop on the desk.

"Right, but it has names like 'Fred Flintstone' in it," Boxer said.

"No addresses or phone numbers, Sam?" Lisa asked.

"Nope. Not even emails. Only aliases."

"How about Maxime? Did she leave behind a client list?" Lisa queried.

"No. She had fewer records than Layla." Boxer shook his head.

"Did he have enemies at his work?" Sam stuck a finger to his chin.

"Good idea. We can follow up on that. Poodles and I have already interviewed some of the employees there," Boxer said. "We can go back and find out where they were when the bomb went off."

"Any other ideas?" Poodles looked around the room. Everyone looked down. "Right. Boxer and I will follow up at Pest-B-Gone. What will you and Lisa do, Sam?"

Sam looked up. "Where's Sebastian's body?"

"They put it in a body bag. It's in the police morgue."

"I'd like a look at it."

"OK, but I hope your stomach is stronger than it has been." Boxer tapped his phone. "Hi, Mildred. I've got some PIs coming over to the morgue. Let them see the body of Sebastian Filmore . . . what's left of it. Thanks." He looked at them. "You're cleared to go."

"Is it in this building?" Sam asked.

"No, the morgue's in Brooklyn."

Sam looked up the address on his phone and then drove over there with Lisa.

The stocky gray-haired manager of the morgue, Mildred Belamy, met them when they entered. "So nice of you to pay us a visit, Mr. and Mrs. Melvin. Mr. Filmore is waiting for you."

"Are you serious?" Lisa asked.

"Never!" she said with a grin. "That's what makes this job enjoyable."

She led them into the chilled room with dozens of drawers in the wall. "E-57, that's Mr. Filmore." She pulled out the drawer. A body bag lay upon it.

"Take as long as you'd like," she said cheerily as she left.

Lisa grabbed the zipper. "You ready, Sam?"

"As ready as I'll ever be." He took a deep breath, which fogged the cold air in front of his face.

Lisa unzipped the bag and opened it up. Four bloody limbs and a head surrounded a hairy torso.

"Oh, that's bad." He looked away and then did a double take. "Huh. Look at that."

"What?"

"The sockets don't match the limbs."

"You're right. So what do you expect after an explosion?"

Sam didn't answer. He stared into space. "You can close it up, Lisa. I've seen enough."

"That was a long drive for five minutes with the body."

"I have an idea. Let's go to our hotel room so I can think about it."

Sam hardly talked to Lisa on their way back to Manhattan. So she worked on the next edition of the *Midley Beacon*. She read it to Sam. She'd left nothing out—the story included blowing up the zombie and pictures of the closed body bag.

"This should get some hits. But it's not dynamic enough to go viral," Lisa said.

Sam just kept his eyes on the busy Long Island Expressway.

Once in the hotel room, Sam settled in front of his laptop and typed furiously.

"Are you coming to bed, Sam?"

"What? Oh, no. I'm trying to figure this out by tomorrow."

"What? The whole zombie murder mystery?"

"Yeah. That's it."

"You've never been a deep thinker, and I've never seen you so driven. I'm worried." Lisa went to bed but didn't pull up the covers.

Sam was staring at his laptop screen when she woke in the morning, still in the same chair.

"Did you stay awake all night?"

"Yup. But it was worth it. I'm ready. I just have to make a few phone calls."

"Who?"

"Chief Detective Dirkse. But first Mildred."

"Why her?"

"She's key to the whole thing."

"I thought she was just a ditsy old broad."

"Ditsy? Nah, just unconventional. I'll shower and then make my calls."

"What about breakfast?"

"After the calls."

"You've never turned down breakfast or even delayed it before. You must have something big."

After his calls, Sam finally relaxed. A huge smile covered his face. "Let's go eat. I'm starving"

At breakfast he devoured steak, eggs, and pancakes. When he leaned back sipping his coffee, she asked, "So what's going on?"

"I've called a meeting at the NYPD headquarters. Chief Detective Dirkse will be there, the three call girls, Boxer, Poodles, us, and of course, Mildred the Morgue Head."

"That's Mildred Belamy."&&

"She laughed when I called her Mildred the Morgue Head this morning."

"She'd laugh at anything. Why is she so important?"

"She has a key part of this mystery. I'll reveal all in the meeting."

"This is like a Nero Wolf or Sherlock Holmes reveal?"

"Exactly, Dr. Kambacher." Sam liked to use Lisa's maiden name to tease her.

"And you won't let me in on it?"

"Do you want to be part of the catastrophe that will happen if I'm wrong?"

"So you could be wrong?"

"Sure. But this feels so right. I'm sure I've got it."

"Now I'm eager for this. When's the meeting?"

"Ten a.m. We've got time to brush our teeth."

Sam and Lisa were the first ones in the conference room, soon followed by Boxer and Poodles.

"What's this all about, Sam?" Poodles frowned at him.

"He didn't even tell me, Poodles. But he thinks he's solved the murder mystery."

"If you have, this'll be the first productive meeting I've been in all year," Boxer said.

The three call girls came in together—Shawna, Bethany, and Vida.

"I hope you have something, Sam. I'm losing my only time to sleep," Vida grumped at him.

"So are we, Vida, and you don't hear us bitching," Bethany said.

Vida flounced in response.

Precisely at ten, Chief Detective Dirkse came in. "Sam, I canceled a meeting with the mayor to make yours. If you've got a solution to this zombie murder, it's worth it. Otherwise, you're fired."

"Don't worry, Chief. The NYPD will come up smelling like roses on this."

"Are we ready to start?"

"No, I'm waiting for Mildred."

"Bellamy? Why do you need her?"

"You'll see."

Mildred Bellamy entered. "The traffic was terrible on the Long Island Expressway. But I'm finally here."

"Was my guess right, Mildred?"

"Spot on."

"Do you have it?"

"Yes."

"Where?"

"In the waiting room."

Sam chuckled. "That's funny. But all the pieces are in place now. Let's begin."

"I've gathered you here today because one of you is a murderer and one is the victim, the last victim."

Everyone looked at each other.

"Poodles was the first one to suspect something wasn't quite right about these zombie murders. She said everything was too obvious. I agreed with her in my gut, but I had no reason."

"Gut instincts are often the best," Poodles said.

"But often wrong," Boxer added.

"In this case, my gut was right. After Sebastian got away, I was sure he'd hang around the apartments, and he did. The fact that he seemed to be a customer of Vida's was significant, but I didn't know why.

"I watched the video of Layla's murder over and over. Layla stopped talking *before* Sebastian tore off her head. That said someone was behind the couch at the time, slicing her neck."

"All you have are wild theories. No evidence," Poodles said.

"Right. No evidence yet. Given the murderer was on the floor hidden by the couch, how did he or she leave? Answer: crawling out the broken window where Sebastian could catch him or her. That's a trivial task for someone with zombie strength. The couch still hid enough of the floor from the security camera."

"So who has the motive to kill Layla and Maxime, regardless of how it was done?" Dirkse asked.

"I'll get to that. But first, let's cover the last victim."

"Who was that?"

"Sebastian. I think he was murdered to cover up the other murders. He was obviously an accomplice to the real murderer."

"How was that done? Somehow a very powerful bomb got in there," Boxer said.

"Through a certain source, I found out the prison cook smuggled in two capsules of nitroglycerin, which Sebastian put together and rolled toward the cell bars. It was much more powerful than he expected."

"Why would the cook do that?"

"The cook was a friend of the murderer, who told him the capsules contained love letters."

"Love letters?"

"Yes. You see, Sebastian and the murderer were in love."

"When we found him hiding in Vida's apartment, it was clear he was more than a customer. He was a friend, a close friend. Isn't that right, Vida?"

"Yeah."

"So why was Vida friendly with a murderer? Which came first, the murders or the love? It had to be the love. So I tracked him through Layla's spreadsheet."

"How? All the names are aliases," Boxer demanded.

"Thanks to Vida. She called Sebastian 'Fred Flintstone.' It so happens that was a name in Layla's spreadsheet. I tracked all his transactions. He mostly saw Vida, but he also saw Layla."

"O-o-oh," Lisa and Poodles said together.

"Get to the point, Sam. I haven't got all day," Chief Dirkse said.

"That established jealousy as a possible motive. I didn't even think of that until my darling wife pointed out to me that Poodles was good looking and a possible rival to her."

"Isn't that obvious, Sam?" Lisa rolled her eyes.

"Not when my eyes and heart are full of you."

"Aw" went the whole room.

"You mushball. Carry on. Get to the point, like the chief says." Lisa looked pleased.

"So if Vida got jealous of Layla, maybe she killed Layla and just used Sebastian to cover it up." Sam looked at Vida.

"You're crazy. I was in my room at the time. There's nothing on the security camera." Vida scowled at Sam.

"Right. That's what took me the longest to figure out. The first question is, why tear off Layla's head and remove it? And Maxime's? I assume Sebastian saw both of them, right, Vida?"

"Who knows? All I know is he loved me."

"But if you cut the carotid artery with a knife, aside from making a ton of blood, it kills very fast."

"I wouldn't know," Vida said.

"And no one else would know if the head was torn off."

"Crazier and crazier."

"So if someone would tear off heads to hide a murder, why not blow up a boyfriend?"

"I loved Sebastian! I'd never kill him." Vida began to cry.

"I'm not sure it was on purpose or merely a miscalculation of the amount of nitroglycerine, but it doesn't matter. You see, we have an eyewitness."

"What?"

"Mildred, call the eyewitness."

"You bet, Sam." She tapped her phone. "It's time."

An orderly wheeled in a body bag on a cart.

"What's this?" Vida asked.

"Who's this?" Chief Dirkse asked.

"Those are the remains of Sebastian Filmore. Open it up, Lisa. You're the one with the strong stomach."

The bag showed a very skinny, clean-shaven guy in dark glasses lying within.

"Is that—" Poodles began.

He sat up and took off the glasses, and zombie-red eyes looked at Vida.

"Sebastian!" Vida rushed toward him.

"Stop her!" Sam yelled.

Boxer grabbed her wrist, which held a very small, very sharp knife. Poodles tackled her.

Everyone talked and babbled at once until Lisa yelled, "Everyone! Shut up! Let Sam finish this."

"Thanks, Lisa. When I saw the stumps of Sebastian's body, unlike the arms, legs, and head, they weren't bleeding. They were covered with skin. Then I knew his zombie bacteria was still working and he'd soon revive."

"That's why he's so skinny," Lisa said.

"Right. The bacteria work off existing body tissue. I called Mildred last night and warned her. He came to this morning, right, Mildred?"

"Right. And he told me the whole story, just as I told you at three a.m."

"So there you have it. Everything's been verified by Sebastian and the cook, who was one of Vida's customers."

"How could you do this to me, Sebastian?" Vida wailed helplessly.

"I love you, Vida, but you're too crazy for me or anyone else. Blowing my head off was a step too far."

"I thought the explosion would just take out the bars. You wouldn't be hurt, since you're a zombie."

"Book her, Boxer, Poodles," Chief Dirkse said.

"On it, chief," Boxer said. He and Poodles dragged her from the room.

"Sam, we paid you a lot of money, but you were worth it. If you ever want a permanent position, we have one for you here in the NYPD."

"Thanks, Chief, but I want to stay in Midley with Lisa."

"Lisa could come with you. We provide relocation service for key management positions."

"My gut tells me it wouldn't be right for me."

"Listen to your gut, Sam," Lisa said.

Chapter 15 – *Midley Beacon*

"We're doing good, Sam," Lisa said on their way back to their hotel room. "Your reports from New York City on the zombie murders have brought in hundreds of thousands of dollars in advertising. C'mon back to the *Midley Beacon*. I've missed you. And it's cheaper now having you on the payroll than paying you a commission for every story. Of course, you will have to take a pay cut. You've lost all seniority and will have to start at the bottom."

"That's OK. It all goes to our income. And I'd work for you for free."

"Don't tempt me. It's only my extreme sense of fairness that forces me to pay you."

"Don't you also claim my salary as a tax deduction?"

"Of course."

"So the more you pay me, the fewer taxes you'll have to pay for the *Midley Beacon*, right?"

"Well yes, but we'll have to pay more personal income taxes. Hell, you've got me doubting what my optimal strategy should be. Let me sit down with my *Midley Beacon* tax spreadsheets and work out the optimal salary to pay you to minimize taxes. It's somewhere between zero and a hundred fifty thousand."

"Whoa! Where did that number come from?"

"That's my salary. I won't pay you more than that. Let's see . . ." Lisa frowned as she pounded furiously on her laptop. The spreadsheet flashed and blinked as it refreshed. Pivot tables flickered, and charts blinked like semaphores.

Once again Sam marveled at her mind. She thought so fast, her typing and spreadsheet updates were just a blur. And she was never in doubt.

"OK. Here it is." Lisa pointed at the intersection of two lines. "That's the solution for minimal taxes and minimal salary expenses. "

"So what is it?"

"Um, seventy-three thousand, one hundred fifty dollars and twenty-three cents. I'll round it to seventy-three thousand."

"Not seventy-four?"

"Nope. But be sure to charge all your expenses to the paper. I'll give you a per diem. I wouldn't mind if you drove the paper's income negative. None of that is taxable. Hmmm. How about the *Midley Beacon* buys your car and lets you use it as a perk?"

"I love that car. What'd be the benefit of that?"

"We'd deduct the purchase price and monthly expense of the car, and you wouldn't have to pay that from your salary. I'll do that with my car too."

"Is that legal?"

"Sure. Free cars are normal corporate perks. Don't sweat it."

"OK, Lisa."

Epilogue – from *My Undead Mother-in-Law*

The next morning Sam Melvin, once again investigative reporter for the print and e-newspaper the *Midley Beacon*, scanned through his daily internet search on "zombie turkeys," "zombie squirrels," "zombie rabbits," "zombie cows," and "zombie humans." The blog post on a dinner with a zombie family startled him. He knew very few humans turned zombie. Of those few, most took the zombie bacteria antibiotic. Almost no news at all surfaced about the few who chose to remain a zombie. He smelled a story.

"Lisa! How would you like a story on zombie humans?" Sam called from his office to hers. Since the *Midley Beacon*'s revenue had exploded through its reporting on the zombie turkey plague, they had expanded their downtown (one street) Midley office from one room to four: an office for him and Lisa (hers was bigger), a reception area for visitors, and an open area for reporters.

"Don't yell from your office!" Lisa yelled from her office. "Zombie humans? Of course, cretin! That would be worth millions of hits. You know perfectly well we're barely scraping by at the *Midley Beacon*. We can't live on zombie squirrel stories forever. Zombie humans would be ideal. But there hasn't been any new news on them!" Lisa paused in her reflexive insulting and asked, "What d'ya got?"

"I have a blog post on a dinner with a zombie family."

"Doesn't sound too interesting, unless they're eating people."

"Nope, pot roast. However, a fight broke out between two zombies, a mother and a son."

"Promising! Who won?"

"The mom. She tore off her son's arm and beat him with it."

"Ouch! I assume it grew back?"

"Yes. I think I should visit this blogger and find out about this family."

"Of course you should! Repost the blog story and tell our readers you'll be investigating it today. Where's the blogger live?"

"He lives in Toledo, but he's traveling. He didn't say where. I think he's hiding something, probably the identity of the family."

"Double-plus good! Get on his good side, and get in contact with the family. Offer to pay him for hits on the blog post from the Midley site."

"I'm on it!"

Read more of this story in My Undead Mother-in-Law. Click here.

My Undead Mother-in-law: The Family Zombie With Anger Management Issues (The Life After Life Chronicles Book 3)

https://www.amazon.com/dp/B0743FQ3QC/

Author Bio

Photo by Barb Lloyd

Andy Zach was born Anastasius Zacharias, in Greece. His parents were both zombies. Growing up, he loved animals of all kinds. After moving to the United States as a child, in high school he won a science fair by bringing toads back from suspended animation. Before turning to fiction, Andy published his PhD thesis "Methods of Revivification for Various Species of the Kingdom Animalia" in the prestigious JAPM, *Journal of Paranormal Medicine.* Andy, in addition to being the foremost expert on paranormal animals, enjoys breeding phoenixes. He lives in Illinois with his five phoenixes.

Join his mailing list here:
https://mailchi.mp/22d3daf2a1b7/get-your-books-byandy-zach

Subscribers get free books from Andy!